Under the Watsons' Porch

SUSAN SHREVE

Under the Watsons' Porch

Alfred A. Knopf · New York

THIS IS A BORZOI BOOK PUBLISHED BY ALFRED A. KNOPF

Text copyright © 2004 by Susan Shreve

Jacket illustration copyright © 2004 by Strauss/Curtis/CORBIS

All rights reserved under International and Pan-American Copyright Conventions. Published in the United States of America by Alfred A. Knopf, an imprint of Random House Children's Books, a division of Random House, Inc., New York, and simultaneously in Canada by Random House of Canada Limited, Toronto. Distributed by Random House, Inc., New York.

KNOPF, BORZOI BOOKS, and the colophon are registered trademarks of Random House, Inc.

www.randomhouse.com/kids

Library of Congress Cataloging-in-Publication Data
Shreve, Susan Richards.
Under the Watsons' porch / Susan Shreve. — 1st ed.
p.   cm.
SUMMARY: Twelve-year-old Ellie's boring summer becomes exciting when she develops a crush on her new next-door neighbor, an older boy with a troubled past, whom her parents have forbidden her to see.
ISBN 0-375-82630-0 (trade) — ISBN 0-375-92630-5 (lib. bdg.)
[1. Friendship—Fiction. 2. Parent and child—Fiction. 3. Summer—Fiction.] I. Title.
PZ7.S55915Un 2004
[Fic]—dc22
2003061383

Printed in the United States of America
July 2004
10 9 8 7 6 5 4 3 2 1
First Edition

For Theo

1. Bored to Death

Today, Saturday, June 6, is my birthday and I'm twelve although I tell people who don't otherwise know me that I'm thirteen, and they believe me. I'm an excellent liar.

It's noon and I'm sitting on our front porch in an Adirondack chair drinking pale lemonade, which looks like white wine, from a long-stemmed wineglass, which I took from the cabinet where my mother keeps her best glasses. My parents are out with my brother, Milo, probably buying me some more birthday presents because they feel terrible. At least my parents do. I had to cancel my birthday party, which was going to be today, because Rosie O'Leary was having hers and her invitations got sent out before mine did and I didn't get one from her. So my friends are at Rosie's party and I'm here.

"Maybe the invitation Rosie sent to you was lost in the mail, Ellie," my mother said, trying, as she always does, to be optimistic.

"Rosie didn't send me an invitation, Mom," I said.

"Oh dear," my mother said in that way she has of speaking when she doesn't know what else to say.

"Never mind," I said. "I don't like Rosie and I'd be bored to death at her stupid birthday party."

My mother agreed especially about Rosie, but later I heard my father say he never did like Mr. O'Leary and my mother replied that all of the O'Learys, including the grandmother, were "predatory," her favorite word this year, so I put a pillow over my ears and pretended to be asleep.

"I hope you'll be okay," my mother said just a little while ago as she left the house with Milo and my father for the shops of Toledo. I waved goodbye and said I was fine, and glad not to have a birthday party of my own and especially not to be at Rosie's.

It's exhausting to be the child of parents who worry as much about your happiness as mine do.

From the bathroom window, I had watched them drive away, then took a shower and put on powder blue shorts and an oversized white tee so the hard sticky-out plums on their way to becoming breasts don't show through the shirt. I put my wet hair in a high ponytail, took the fancy wineglass, and that's how I happen to be on the front porch making a list of my special enemies at Duncan Middle School when Tommy Bowers walks out of the yellow house next door.

I catch sight of him trotting down the steps out of the corner of my eye, his hands in the pockets of his trousers, wearing a starchy white shirt with the sleeves rolled up and his long black hair floppy across his forehead.

I'm thinking he'll stop, look in my direction, and call out to me.

"What are you doing?" I'm hoping he will ask.

"Just drinking white wine and writing a poem to my boyfriend in South Africa," I'll say, asking him to come up on the front porch and join me.

But he's on his way up the street and I don't think I caught his attention, so there's no chance of talking now.

I don't know Tommy Bowers. This is the first time I've even seen him, but I've heard all about him. All I really know is that the day before yesterday he moved into the yellow house next door with Mr. and Mrs. Bowers—her name is Clarissa—and their old calico cat, Bounce, who is missing an ear. We live in a gossipy neighborhood and people have been talking about the Bowerses ever since they bought the yellow house. Especially they've been talking about Tommy.

"The Bowerses are older parents," my mother confides in me as if she's already become friends with them even though they've never met. "And I understand Tommy's a handful."

"Handful" is my grandmother's word and she usually uses it about me. As if I could fit in anyone's hand, especially my tiny grandmother's.

I lean against the porch railing watching Tommy Bowers walk up the street full of confidence, a little swing to his walk as if he's always lived here.

Our house is gray shingle in the middle of a block that slopes upward in the direction of Tommy's yellow house, which is next to the Brittles and their twin boys. On the other side of the Brittles is the Watsons' house. The largest house on the block, it's at the top of the street on the corner of Lincoln Road, which is the name of our street, and Jefferson Place.

The Watsons are very old sisters who live alone, and I've almost never seen them. There used to be another Watson sister but she got carried out of the house in a box and the neighborhood kids watched, including Milo and me but not the Brittle twins because their parents wouldn't let them. Four men carried the box down the front steps and put it in the back of a long black car and drove away. The other Watson sisters stood on the porch, their hands folded in front of them, so I know they're tall and skinny and could die at any time, according to Milo, who is interested in these sorts of things and so had an especially good time watching the box come out of the house with the dead Miss Watson in it.

When I look up the hill, I see that Tommy has stopped in front of the Watsons'. He's standing, one shoulder higher than the other, looking up, and he may be talking to someone on the porch but I can't see that far even though I'm leaning over the railing so my stomach is almost sliced in half. I can't see his face although it looks as if he's wearing glasses and now he's folded his arms across his chest.

So I climb up on the railing in order to see the Watsons' porch, which is impossible to see lying on my stomach, and as I do, Tommy looks toward me and raises his hand.

Just the slightest motion as if we're already friends and

have a secret code. Which is enough of an invitation for me on my birthday.

I hop off the railing, brush the black dirt off my blue shorts, take the rubber band out of my wet ponytail, and shake my long dark hair so it's as floppy as his. Then, barefooted, I run down the steps with a kind of excitement I used to have on my birthday when I was little and actually believed something different was about to happen because it was my birthday.

Ever since Christmas this year, I've felt as carved and empty as a jack-o'-lantern. I look in the mirror on the back of my mother's closet door and my face seems to have fallen into itself, becoming the face of someone else, broader across the cheeks, the teeth too big in my mouth, my hips spreading so jeans that used to slip over my hips like a pillowcase leave rolls of flesh over the waistband when I try to pull them on. And that's only what happens in front of the mirror.

In the morning when the alarm goes off in Milo's room, I don't want to get up, as if already the day has been too long and it hasn't even started. At school, especially in art, which I hate because I'm not good with my hands, I look up from whatever project I'm working on with the feeling that someone like Rosie O'Leary is rolling her eyes at me and laughing. And sometimes after school, my mother still at work, Milo at a friend's, I let myself in the front door and flop into the big cushy chair in the living room where my parents used to read to me, and I sit staring at nothing, with this long sadness covering me from head to toe.

I know about sadness, like when my Uncle Walter died, and when Blue Tip, the cat my parents had since before I was born, died, and when my best friend, Lynny Brady, moved to England after first grade, and the summer my parents made me go to sleepaway camp for six weeks because my mother was having an operation.

But this sadness is different. Nothing bad happens to me but the sadness comes creeping over my shoulder like an insect. Sometimes it just floats away, and other times it hangs out driving me crazy until I do something. Go on a bike ride to the high school or make chocolate chip brownies or call up my friend P.J. to talk about the girls in our class and whether they've gotten their period. And always lately, the funny sadness is sleeping just below the surface of my skin, especially since the Maypole dance when I didn't get chosen and had to be in the chorus instead of the dance, singing "Welcome to the joys of May-ay-ay" like some first grader with my mouth wide open so the sound would carry.

It's as if I'm waiting for something but I don't know what it is and so I can't go after it.

When I get to the Watsons' house, Tommy is leaning down next to the side porch examining the latticework that covers the area under the porch.

"Hi," I call from the sidewalk. "Are you Tommy Bowers?"

"Nope," he says without looking up. He's fooling with something on the lattice.

"Yes you are," I say, walking up the driveway. "You just moved in next door to my house."

"I did just move in next door to your house," he says.

"So." I stand next to him and see that he is trying to unlock a very rusty hook and eye so the lattice, which is also a door, will swing back and we can walk under the porch.

"There," he says, pulling at the lattice so it opens and stepping under the porch. "Cool."

The Watsons' porch is very high, much higher than ours, and very long, wrapping all the way around three sides of the house. Someone Tommy's height—and he's taller than I am by a lot—can walk under the porch without ducking, into a huge dark room with a dirt floor and light filtering through the lattice so there're triangles of light making a design on the dirt floor.

"My name is Ellie Tremont."

He's standing in the middle of the dirt room looking around, appraising.

"Who lives in this house?" he asks finally.

"The Watson sisters," I say. "They're old."

"Good." He takes a pack of cigarettes out of the pocket of his trousers and offers me one.

"I don't smoke," I say, but I'm very excited. No one has ever offered me a cigarette and it makes me feel very old and smart.

"I just carry cigarettes and candy to make friends." He offers me some peanut M&M's, which I take.

"So who are you if not Tommy Bowers?" I ask.

"Tom Cruise," he says matter-of-factly.

I don't argue.

"This place will make a great hideout. We've got to decide what we're going to do with it."

"Who's we?" I ask.

"You and me," he says, walking around the side of the house.

"You don't think there're rats under here, do you?"

"Not a lot," he says. "I'll take care of you if one comes slinking around."

I can't believe my ears, some boy taking care of me and

I'm twelve years old and almost without thinking, I just ask him how old he is and he says thirteen.

"Me too," I say just as easily as if it were true. "Today."

"Today is your birthday?"

I nod.

"So let's go have a party at your house and decide what to do with the Watsons' porch."

"I was sitting on the porch drinking wine when I saw you," I say, very happy with the way this day is turning out.

Tommy locks the lattice door and we walk down the driveway, down the street to my house, and I fill two wine-glasses with lemonade so we can sit on the front porch together and smoke Tommy's unlit cigarettes until my parents and Milo get home with the presents.

2. True Stories

Tommy sits down on one of the Adirondack chairs, puts his feet up on the porch railing, folds his arms across his chest, and surveys the neighborhood.

I am sitting across from him rolling the stem of the wineglass between my fingers as I've seen my father do, watching Tommy take a sip of lemonade.

"I thought you were drinking wine," he says, looking over at me.

"I was," I say without smiling. "But I finished it."

"And there isn't any more?"

I shake my head. Not sure whether he knows that I'm not telling the truth. Maybe he always drinks wine when he wants to. Maybe he's allowed to do anything he chooses.

"So we've got to think about the Watsons' porch."

"I think it's creepy under there."

"Creepy's good." He has a thoughtful look on his face, his brow wrinkled, his lips tight. He looks older than other boys I know—not in his face, exactly, but in the way he moves and sits, the way he crosses his legs and rests his head against his hand.

"What I'm thinking is that we could do something with the kids in the neighborhood, just you and me. Something exciting." He puts an unlit cigarette in his mouth and takes a drag. "I'd like the kids in this neighborhood to know who I am."

"What do you mean?" I ask. "Like, know your name?"

"I'd like them to *know* me."

I don't understand what he means about kids knowing him and why he even cares. I sometimes think about whether or not the big kids like me and mostly they don't even know I'm alive. But in this neighborhood, there are mostly little kids.

"Well, there're a lot of kids around here, especially little ones," I say.

"Good," he says. "What I like about little kids is that you can tell them anything and they believe you."

"What are you thinking of telling them?" I asked.

He was quiet for a minute, probably thinking, and then he shrugged.

"I haven't decided what I want to tell them yet until we figure out what to do under the Watsons' porch."

It's hilly where we live and our house is set high over the street, so I can sit on my front porch like we're doing now and watch the kids going into and coming out of their houses all day in the summer. It's a quiet neighborhood and safe, so safe that on our block the kids, even the little ones, are allowed to wander up and down the street, into and out of each other's houses, without a grown-up. That's why my parents moved here, because, as they tell me all the time, they want me to be free. The houses here are small, "starter" houses, my dad says, a place to start a family and then when the kids are older they move to a neighborhood with bigger houses. We still live here even though I'm older, because there's only me and Milo and my parents are teachers and can't afford a big house. So mostly the families here are starter families with smaller kids and I plan to tell Tommy about every one of them.

"How many kids do you think live on this street?"

"There're a lot. Fourteen of them—eleven not counting the babies."

I happen to know this because every year we give a Christmas party and my mother and I make gingerbread girls and boys for each child and write his or her name across the gingerbread bellies in white icing.

"There's Billy and Sarah Block, across the street in the yellow brick house, and they fight a lot but I like them okay," I begin. "And then Hannah Joseph next door to the Blocks and she's an only child and sort of whiney. And Sean and Cara and Ian O'Shaunessey live in the last house, the one with the big fence that keeps their vicious German shepherd from biting anyone. My mom calls them *stairsteps* because they're six and seven and eight."

Tommy finishes his lemonade, takes a drag of his unlit cigarette.

"The Brittles have twin boys called Alexander and Anthony and they're seven and kind of bullies because their parents are so particular—that's what Mom says—and there's Miranda Salon next door to us, who's five, and her parents are divorced, so she lives with her mother and grandmother, and Lisa and Jonathan Bellman, who live on the corner."

"That's it?"

"That's it."

"Except your brother."

"Milo."

Tommy gets up from the Adirondack chair, walks to the edge of the porch, and checks down the street, looking at something; then he tells me he wants to see the house.

"Why do you want to see *my* house?" I ask.

"I just do," he says with unusual formality, as if he were as old as my father and accustomed to politeness the way grown-ups are. "I have an interest in houses."

"Sort of like an architect?"

"No," he says. "I like houses because they're places to live."

He says this seriously as if it makes a lot of sense. I have no idea what he means but I can tell what he's said is important, so I decide not to say anything at all, especially anything funny.

I love stories, which is probably why I make them up so often, and if you listen, you get to know the secret stories of people. I have a sense that Tommy Bowers is full of secret stories.

"Our house is nothing special," I say. "And besides, it's a mess. My mom would kill me for taking a guest around when it's such a disaster."

This house where I was born—and so was Milo—is perfectly ordinary except for being old, with none of what my mother calls "the conveniences." There's a living room and dining room and kitchen and four bedrooms and a screened-in sunporch that goes off my bedroom, where I have sleepovers in the summer since we don't have air-conditioning. Air-conditioning is one of the conveniences we do without because my father is a schoolteacher in junior high and my mother teaches drama at the high school, and schoolteachers don't have "the extras," which include, according to my mother, two cars and two television sets and private telephones for the children and summer vacations at resorts or winter vacations at ski lodges and new slipcovers for the living room. I don't care about these things but Milo and my mother do, so it's a subject for discussion at the dinner table, usually introduced by Milo when one of his friends has gotten a new bicycle or video or skateboard. "I want . . ." is how the conversation begins, and that is followed either by "You can't have . . ." or "We can't afford. . . ." And sometimes, to my satisfaction, there's the comment, usually from my father, that begins, "Ellie doesn't always say, 'I want. . . .' " Which is perfectly true.

But there is something I do want. I just don't bring the subject up to my parents because it would make them unhappy, and besides, they probably know it already, the way parents seem to know everything whether you tell them or not.

The truth is I would like to have been asked to Rosie O'Leary's birthday party and then I could have said, "Thank you very much but I'm afraid that I'm unable to come, even in time for birthday cake, because it would bore me to death."

In my class of twenty-seven girls and fifteen boys, almost the same class I've been with since I started kindergarten, sixteen of the girls are popular and the rest of us are hopeless. "Hopeless" is P.J.'s word.

"It's not a bad thing," P.J. said to me. "It's just the way it is when you're a girl and doomed."

The popular girls in the sixth grade dress alike in tight jeans and little T-shirts with flowers in full bloom painted on the back and clunky shoes. They come to school with a stash of makeup hidden in their bookbags, and in the girls' room before school begins, they spread peach blush on their cheekbones, paint their nails magenta, and put lavender eye shadow on their eyelids.

And they whisper. It's the whispering I especially don't like.

I would rather be doomed than popular, but I'd like to make the choice myself.

So I've become very good at lying. "Safe lies" is how I think of them. I'll say things casually, like, "We'll be going to Vail, Colorado, to ski for Christmas as usual." Or "I have a cousin who is an actress in New York City (which is true) and she has given me a walk-on part in her television show (which is not true)." Or that I have a boyfriend in South Africa whom I met on my summer vacation.

And if I'm asked about my grades—a subject the popular sixteen girls are interested in discussing—I say, "mostly A's and an F." I like that balance. It makes me seem smart and a little dangerous. Hardly anyone gets an F.

Tommy goes through the screen door and into the hall, standing in the middle of the room, which is small but with enough space for my grandmother's old gold brocade loveseat with springs that stick in your bottom if you happen to sit down on it, which we don't.

"So is this all you have downstairs?" Tommy asks. "Just three rooms?"

"We have a bathroom downstairs. A half bathroom." As if that information will hold any interest for Tommy.

"Powder room," he says. "That's what the mother I had before this one called the downstairs bathroom. We had two powder rooms in the mansion where we lived, one for guests."

He heads for the kitchen and I follow him.

What I know of Tommy's history is complicated and I don't know if it's true. My father, who wouldn't dream of making up stories, told me that Tommy was a "doorstep baby" when doorstep babies were more common.

"He was left by someone, maybe his real mother, maybe not, on the doorstep of an older woman's house who hadn't the wherewithal to deal with a baby and so she called the authorities." That's how my father talks. As old-fashioned as if he were actually my grandfather and he's only thirty-nine.

The authorities, according to my father, are the people in charge of protecting children from bad or incompetent parents. The authorities arranged for Tommy to live with Betty something or other and her husband, but Betty turned out to be incompetent, leaving Tommy in his baby carriage in front of the S&F department store so she could go inside to look for leather pants, which took her several hours. I know Tommy had a second mother before he went to live with Clarissa Bowers, but my father didn't know the details of those stories. Besides, he said, it's hard to know what's true and what isn't. No one I've ever met has had so many mothers.

"So what kind of mansion did you live in?" I ask.

I've never been inside a mansion and we don't have any in our neighborhood. But there is the Slough Mansion downtown, where you can pay five dollars to the Slough family to take a look around on Saturdays and Sundays when it's open, and the Birdsall Mansion near the high school, which is a private art gallery, but I've never been to either one.

"A huge mansion and I didn't like it," Tommy says. "It was in Florida and I lived there with Belinda and Jack and their 'natural' son, Jack junior. They had big cats." He opened the fridge.

"Big cats?" I ask.

"Tigers, jaguars, that kind of thing. They were big-game hunters in Zimbabwe." He took a bottle of white wine, Pinot Grigio, from the inside shelf of the fridge where my parents keep it. "May I have some?" he asks, perfectly normal, as if it is the most ordinary thing in the world to come into my house and open my fridge and take out a bottle of white wine.

And I say yes. I'm sitting on the kitchen table with my legs crossed yoga-style and my arms folded across my chest and thinking to myself that I've just said yes to a thirteen-year-old boy's drinking my parents' wine. I must have a worried expression on my face because Tommy looks over at me with a sweet smile.

"Don't worry," he says. "I'm allowed to drink wine whenever I want at home."

"Me too," I say, though of course this isn't true.

Milo and I are allowed to have a sip of wine, usually champagne, at Christmas dinner and Thanksgiving and sometimes at my parents' birthdays, but it's only a sip poured in the bottom of our glass and it has never oc-curred to me, never even crossed my mind, to try it myself from the open bottle my parents keep in the refrigerator.

Something about Tommy Bowers makes me *want* to say yes to everything he asks. He could ask me to run away from home with him or skip school or take a nap in my parents' bed, which even I'm not allowed to do. And I'd probably say yes. I'm thinking that this could be the rule of our friendship from now on. Sitting here in the old kitchen of our dumpy house watching him pour Pinot Grigio in my mother's very best wineglass, I am thinking that I may always say yes to Tommy.

"Did the tigers and jaguars live in cages?" I change the subject.

"They were dead," he says opening the back door and looking out at our garden, which is my mother's pride and joy, with roses and camellias and lilac bushes and a cutting garden.

"They kept them mounted on the wall. Just their heads. The jaguar's tongue was hanging out when they killed him." He turns to me and smiles, a toothy smile with a dimple on one side of his mouth, which makes him look innocent although it's perfectly clear that he's not.

I check the clock. One o'clock. My parents could be home at any time, and they'll be upset to find me in our house with a boy they don't know. In fact, my mother might be crazy mad.

"Where're your parents?" Tommy says as if he's got X-ray vision and can read my thoughts.

"They're buying me a birthday present," I say.

"Do you know what they're going to buy you?" He's sitting at the kitchen table.

"I said I wanted a jean skirt and a new wallet."

"Is that what you really want or just what you said?" he asks.

I'm surprised at his question. It's as if he already knows me better than anyone, even my parents. What I really want is a necklace that I saw at a funky shop called Wake Up Little Suzie. It has three rows of tiny little sparkly diamonds, not real of course but very beautiful. But I didn't ask my parents for it because my mother would say it was a frivolous gift when there are things I really need, like new shoes and a bathing suit.

"What I really want," I tell Tommy, who's on his way out of the kitchen, "is this necklace I saw yesterday in a shop in town."

"What kind?"

"Diamonds," I say.

I'm following Tommy upstairs. He wants to see the bedrooms and I'm thinking, Oh no, I didn't make my bed and I've got underclothes all over the floor, even this new underwire bra that just killed when I wore it to the last day of school yesterday.

"Real?"

I don't answer. All I'm thinking about is what's on the floor of my bedroom.

"How come you don't have any posters?" he asks, going in the door to my bedroom while I run around gathering up the Little Lady blue panties I've left half under the bed and the bra that is on my desk chair and toss them and a couple of T-shirts in my closet.

"I like a lot of posters all over my walls."

I finish collecting the laundry, toss it in the corner of my closet, and collapse at the end of my bed.

"My mom made this girly room when I was about nine,

even the curtains and the bedspread, and I don't complain about it because it'd hurt her feelings," I say.

He has opened the door to the sunporch.

"This is cool," he says.

"I have sleepovers here in the summer."

"We could have a walkie-talkie going from my bedroom to your bedroom." He points to the back of the Bowerses' house. "That's my bedroom."

Tommy's house is modernized, and what used to be a sunporch like mine is now Tommy's bedroom, a glassed-in, heated room so close to my sunporch that I could almost reach over from here to the Bowerses' house and touch it.

"Then we could talk all the time, even when I'm in bed. I'd just call you up and you'd be in bed and we'd talk all night."

"Maybe," I say. "But my mom's a monster about the phone after nine at night."

"That's why we'd have a walkie-talkie. Our mothers would never know."

I'm sitting on the end of my bed and Tommy's looking out the window that faces the house next door, and he turns to me with a quizzical expression on his face.

"What do you think of your mom?"

"I love her," I say, taken aback. "Why do you ask that?"

He shrugs. "You called her a monster as if you don't like her."

"I didn't mean to," I say. "I love her but she also drives me crazy because she's—I don't know—such a mother."

He sits down on the bed beside me.

"I guess I just never had a mother for long enough to know."

"I guess," I say, sounding stupid in my own ears.

But it's hard for me to imagine trying out new mothers since I have always had my funny, flashy-tempered mother, who is a constant in my life, always there whether I want her to be or not.

Tommy has hopped up now and wants to see the rest of the house: Milo's room and the study, my parents' bedroom, and the attic where we keep all of my mom's parents' old furniture since they moved to an apartment, and boxes of my parents' scrapbooks. But I hear my parents' car out front.

"We can't," I say. "My parents will be back soon."

My parents have never said I'm not allowed to have a boy upstairs when no one is in the house. But I know that's what they'll say if they come in the house now and discover that Tommy and I have been in my bedroom together.

That's one of the problems with parents who teach school. Other parents may think their kids are perfect, but my parents know better. They spend all day and night with kids, and according to my mom, none of them is perfect.

Now Tommy has taken a picture of me out of the bookcase. It's my favorite: I was three with curly brown hair, riding on a merry-go-round, my head thrown back, my hands high on the horse's mane as if he's real and I'm in control.

"You?" he asks.

I nod.

"Can I have it?"

"I don't think I can give it to you," I say, wondering what in the world does Tommy Bowers want with a picture of me when I was little.

"I hear my parents' car," I say.

"So we better go downstairs."

"In a hurry," I say.

My parents haven't met Tommy Bowers, only by reputation, but already I have a sense that they're not going to like him.

3. Shadows

I love my bedroom, especially at night, when shadows from the trees bending with the wind and cars taking a shortcut down our street slide across the wall in animal shapes. My bed is wide and high, with a canopy and curtains that pull on either side so I can, as I did when I was little, sleep here totally concealed from anyone who happens to come into my bedroom unannounced. A burglar is the sort of person I imagined coming into my room when I was younger. Milo lies in bed waiting for pit bulls with plans to eat him.

I love that my room is old-fashioned, that it doesn't look like the rooms of my friends who *do* have posters on the walls, mainly rock stars or movie stars, but P.J. has a huge poster of a Labrador retriever, and Linsay, another friend of mine, has James Dean straddling his motorcycle with a cigarette hanging between his lips.

What I have instead of posters is pictures of women in advertisements for Ivory Snow and Lysol and Castile soap and Betty Crocker cake mix. My mother used to have these same pictures in her bedroom when she was growing up, and before that my grandmother had them as well. It makes me feel safe to sleep in a room with pictures that have lasted for so long surrounding my bed.

Maybe I'll explain this to Tommy the next time he mentions posters.

It's after midnight now, going on the day after my birthday, and I'm in bed with a flashlight and a notebook writing a letter to Tommy under my covers, my door shut, my radio tuned to the all-music station on low.

I'm too excited to sleep.

"I haven't seen you so thrilled about your birthday since you were little, Ellie," my mother said at my birthday dinner, which was roast chicken and gravy and mashed potatoes and apple spice cake with maple sugar icing.

"That's because she loves her blue jean skirt," Milo said, since he's the one who gave me the blue jean skirt although my mother picked it out and paid for it.

"I do love it. It makes me look thin again," I said.

"Are you fat?" Milo asked, looking up from his plate.

"Ellie is not fat," my father said. "She's gorgeous."

The truth is I'm regular and used to be skinny, but all of the girls in sixth grade, especially the popular girls, talk about weight and boys, one subject or the other *all* of the time unless it's the end of the grading period and then they talk about grades. So I can't help talking about fat sometimes.

"Maybe Ellie's just happy to be twelve," my mother said. "That would be my guess."

"I'm very happy to be twelve," I said after blowing out the candles on the spice cake, but I'm really neither happy nor unhappy to be twelve. Twelve is fine. It's what I happen to be.

After dinner, we sat around and played Cranium on the dining room table and we always figure out a way to let Milo win because he loses his temper and throws all the game pieces on the floor if he doesn't. When it got to be about ten o'clock, P.J. called from Rosie O'Leary's birthday slumber party to say she was having the most boring time. I could tell as soon as I picked up the phone and heard her whispery voice.

"Is the party terrible?" I ask, hoping that it is since I'm not there.

"The worst," P.J. says. "We had hot dogs and hamburgers and carrot cake, and Josie Tree threw up her cake on Mrs. O'Leary's carpet, so the carpet has to be professionally cleaned and Mrs. O'Leary had a temper tantrum."

"Because of Josie?"

"Because Josie ruined the carpet," P.J. says. "You're lucky you missed it."

"I didn't exactly miss it," I say. "I wasn't invited."

P.J. laughs. "That was lucky, too."

I was really feeling great as I got ready for bed, swinging around a little to the music on the radio, checking to see if Tommy was visible in the bedroom next door. But because my light was on, I couldn't tell.

After I got into bed and turned out my light, pretending I was going to sleep, my mother and father came in together to tell me good night. This didn't surprise me. They often come in together, and on my birthday, every single birthday since I can remember, they sit down on the end of my bed and my mother tells me about the dinner my grandmother brought to the hospital to celebrate the night I was born. The dinner was roast chicken and gravy and mashed potatoes and apple spice cake and even though I didn't get to eat it that night when I was zero, we have had it every June 13 since then.

But tonight my parents had something else in mind.

Even before my father started to speak, I could tell they were going to talk about Tommy.

"Did you meet our new neighbor today?" was the first question.

My parents are hopeless at lying. Of course they *knew* I had met Tommy Bowers. They probably even saw him as he dashed out our back door and over the fence.

As soon as I heard the car door slam, I headed downstairs first so I'd be in the kitchen pretending to check out the fridge when they walked in the front door. Tommy ran down the stairs after me, through the dining room, passing the big window that overlooks the driveway where the car was parked, into the kitchen, out the back door, and over the fence, which goes from our beautiful garden to the Bowerses' ugly one.

I watched through the side window in the kitchen as my parents unpacked the car, came up the front steps, and opened the door, and I could hear Milo stomp up the stairs to my parents' room carrying my presents. My parents could possibly have seen Tommy but they didn't mention it.

Sometime after dinner, Clarissa Bowers called my mother to say how nice it was that Tommy had met me and that I lived next door and how much she hoped that we would be friends, especially since Tommy was new in the neighborhood.

"Mrs. Bowers didn't mention a thing about the trouble Tommy has been in," my father said. "But we learned quite a lot today when we were having coffee at Moxie's sitting at the table next to the Brittles."

"I don't like the Brittles." I slid down in my bed.

"This is about Tommy and not the Brittles," my mother said.

"I just wanted to be clear that I hate them and tonight is still my birthday."

My father put his hand on my leg and said something like "Of course, darling" and "We'd never bring this up if it weren't for your protection" and "We only have your interest at heart." He should know better than to say those things to me, his only daughter. He's a junior high school teacher!

So depending on whether or not you want to believe the Brittles, the story is this:

Thirteen and a half years ago, Tommy was born in Coral Gables, Florida, to a teenage mother who wasn't married, and she gave birth to him in a motel room and left him there. He became a ward of the state of Florida, which located a foster mother and father who did turn out to be more or less like the weirdos Tommy told me about today, with dead jaguars and tigers hanging on their walls. They wanted Tommy because they had a child already, their own, Jack Junior, and they weren't going to have any more children and Jack Junior needed a playmate. Tommy lived with the weirdos until they moved to Germany forever and couldn't take a foster child without adopting him legally, so at nine years old, Tommy was once again a ward of the state of Florida.

For a while, he lived in different foster homes in Florida, getting into more and more trouble, stealing or fighting or skipping school—"minor infractions," my father said, whatever that means.

Not terrible trouble, nothing like guns or killing, but trouble enough that the state put him in a kind of halfway house.

"An orphanage," my mother called it.

Clarissa Bowers, who lived with Mr. Bowers in another part of Toledo close to the river, was looking for a baby.

She had tried to have one of her own and it hadn't worked out. Then one afternoon she was reading a story about foster children in the *Toledo Dispatch* and the idea came to her that since she was getting quite old, almost forty-five, she could adopt a child. Maybe even a troubled child.

"And that's Tommy." My mother was sitting on the end of the bed and even in the darkness I could tell she had that look on her face, her eyes squinty, her mouth puckered as if she were thinking with her lips.

"The Bowerses got him four years ago and he's been quite a handful," my father said.

"So what are you trying to tell me?" I asked. "Not to be friends with him because he's had a miserable, terrible, awful, cruel life and I should only be friends with the lucky people?"

"We're not saying you *can't* spend time with Tommy Bowers," Mom said. "Only that you should be careful."

"I like him," I said quietly, pulling up my covers over the bottom half of my face so only my eyes showed. "I like him better than I've liked anyone I've met for a very long time."

From where I'm lying I can see Tommy Bowers's room. There are two long windows on either end of my room and three smaller windows set high from which I can't see out unless it's night and the Bowers house is lit and I'm lying on my bed.

Now I can see Tommy because he's standing on his bed trying to stick something to the ceiling. I can't tell what it is that he has in his hand but I can tell that he's not having any luck with his project. He keeps jumping on the bed to reach the ceiling, where the overhead light hangs. All I can see in the frame of my window is Tommy's head with his floppy hair, his arms swinging in the air, the four posts of his bed, and the ceiling. I get out of bed and go out on the sunporch to check if I can see more from there. It's a cool night with a full moon, the sky clear and splashed with stars, very beautiful, and I'm thinking how nice it will be to have Tommy living next door. Every night I'll be able to turn out my light and see him in his bedroom or go out on the sunporch and watch him at his desk, which is visible in the window when I'm standing on the sunporch like I am now.

I go back into the bedroom to get the blanket at the bottom of my bed and wrap it around my shoulders so I won't be too cold standing on the sunporch, and as I return to my station across from his room, I hear him call me.

"Ellie!"

I can't make out his face but he must have opened the window and seen me and now I see him hanging out the window with something in his hand.

"Hi." I say it softly.

"I'm trying to make a walkie-talkie for us to use."

"What were you doing jumping on your bed?"

"You saw me?" This pleases him. "Trying to change the light bulb. You'd know everything about me if I could get the walkie-talkie fixed up. Can you come over?"

"It's too late."

I'm thinking my parents won't ever let me go over to Tommy Bowers's house but of course I don't tell Tommy anything like that.

Tommy opens the window wider and climbs out onto the ledge, one leg hanging down the side of the house, the other leg in his bedroom. He is leaning precariously toward me.

"So I've decided what we can do with the Watsons' porch but I don't want to shout it out loud in the neighborhood."

"Whisper it," I say, shivering under my blanket on the cold sunporch.

"I don't want to whisper it either. We'll meet under the Watsons' porch tomorrow morning at about ten."

"I can't," I say. "I have church."

"Church?"

"I mean, I don't have to go to church." Whether it's true or not, I want Tommy to believe I make my own decisions. So I'm thinking I have Sunday school tomorrow at nine-thirty until eleven and then church, so my parents will drop me off tomorrow at Sunday school, First Congregational, about a mile from our house, and I'll tell them I won't be meeting them at church because I want to see P.J., which won't completely surprise them. I'll go into the front door of the church, duck into the girls' room until my parents drive off, and then I'll be on my way down Miler's Road to meet Tommy at ten o'clock. That will give me three hours before my parents get home from church with Milo and we go to Sunday lunch at my grandmother's house.

Our life is so regular, sometimes I wish we lived in a place where there were tornadoes, like Kansas, where my mother grew up.

Tommy waves goodbye, closes the window, and I watch him cross the room, open a desk drawer, and take out something. Then he walks out of view of the sunporch and the windows where I can see him from my bed. I wait, watching, but he has disappeared.

*   *   *

I'm lying in bed again, writing my letter to Tommy—actually thinking about my letter since so far I've written only:
Dear Tommy,

I'm SO excited you have moved in next door. Never in my life have I had a friend with such a huge imagination—the same size as my imagination, which my parents tell me is "dangerously out of control."

I have in mind to say how much I like him and am hoping we'll be best friends but I don't want to seem *too* excited and I especially don't want to sound mushy. So I'm lying half under my covers with my flashlight on, rereading what I've written so far when I think I hear my name.

"Ellie?"

"El?"

At first I think it must be my parents calling although by now it's almost eleven-thirty and they turn out their light at exactly eleven. I open the door to my bedroom and listen.

I hear it again, this time louder. "Ellie." And I can tell it's coming from outside, so I go to the sunporch again and there's Tommy hanging out the window, calling my name.

"Are you crazy?" I laugh.

"I just wanted you to know I put a birthday present for you on your front porch. It's not very well wrapped."

I can't believe he got me a birthday present and we've hardly known each other for a full day. But I'm smiling all over, even my hair is smiling.

"Go downstairs and get it," he says. "I want you to have it before it's tomorrow."

"Okay," I say.

"And then tell me if you like it. I'll be lying in the dark in my room with the window wide open waiting for you to call me."

It takes me a while before I dare leave my bedroom without getting caught.

First Milo comes out of his room, goes into the bathroom, pees leaving the door open, and then goes into my parents' room to wake them up. I'm standing in the doorway to my bedroom with the door almost closed, a tiny slip of space so I can see what is going on in the hall.

I hear some conversation and then my mother walks Milo back to his room, holding his hand, telling him that pit bulls don't live in the neighborhood and if they did, they have no skill whatsoever at getting into locked houses. She stays for a minute in Milo's room and then pads barefoot down the hall. I see her as she passes my door and hear her open her door and shut it but not tight. There is no click.

So I wait a few more minutes just to make sure the pit bulls aren't planning another visit to Milo's room.

We don't have carpet on our stairs, so I walk down very slowly, putting my feet gently, gently down on the wood floor. There are narrow windows on either side of our front door and peering through one, I can see under the porch light that Tommy has left a pink package about the size of a shoebox by the door.

I wait, listening for noises upstairs in case my parents are still awake, and hearing none, I open the front door very quietly and it squeaks like a long, drawn-out guinea pig squeal and I hold my breath, listening. But upstairs is silent.

The present is a mess. It's wrapped in stiff, glossy pink paper, too much of it for the size of the shoebox, with lots of tape at either end, a yellow ribbon with a lopsided bow, and a card with "ELLIE" on the front.

I close the front door.

The whole time I've been downstairs I've heard nothing but the squeak of the front door. The moon, visible in the living room window, is a full pale yellow circle and light pours in the windows on either side of the front door.

At the top step of our stairs, I see Milo sitting on the second step, his hand on the railing, his thumb, even though he's six years old this year, stuck in his mouth.

"What're you doing?" he asks.

"I got a present," I say, quickly inventing a story for this occasion.

"In the middle of the night?"

"It's not even midnight."

"Can I see the present?" Milo asks.

"In the morning. I'm not going to open it now."

Which isn't true, but I certainly don't want Milo to know that I got a present from Tommy Bowers. He'll tell our parents and that will be that.

"You should open it tonight because tomorrow it won't be your birthday anymore."

"That's true," I say. "But I'm going to wait until tomorrow anyway."

I'm hurrying up the stairs past Milo, who moves his little legs so I can pass, and just as I start to go into my bedroom door, my mother comes out into the hall. I pay no attention to her, hoping to be able to get into my room, hide Tommy's present under the bed, and climb under my covers before Milo has a chance to tell her I had a present on the front porch.

But I hear him tell her as they walk down the hall to his room again.

"Ellie came down to get a present that was on the front

porch," he says, "and I still can't sleep because of the pit bulls."

I lie very still. In the Bowers house, I can see the top of Tommy's head and the head of Clarissa Bowers. They are standing beside Tommy's bed and they must be talking, and then Clarissa Bowers disappears from view and so does Tommy, and the light in his bedroom goes out.

Then I hear my mother in the hall outside my door, hear my door open, and she says, "Ellie? Are you awake?"

"A little," I say.

"Milo said you got a present on the front porch."

"Uh-huh," I say. "From P.J. I'll open it in the morning."

4. The Lollipop Garden

My mom is staying in Milo's room forever. I can hear her talking and Milo is whimpering—he's an expert at whimpering—and it'll be hours before I can open Tommy's present, which I stuffed under the bed. Outside I hear sirens, probably a fire from the sound of them, close by our house, which means Milo could be awake all night. Fires and pit bulls are his favorite emergencies. I'm lying in the dark watching the pitch blackness out the window where Tommy's house is, waiting for everyone to go to sleep.

I've almost given up waiting when I hear my mother's

bare feet padding on the hardwood floor on the way to her bedroom. I know she'll stop at my door, open it without knocking as if I'm still six and *need* to be kissed good night, which I don't. She'll call "Ellie?" in her whispery voice. "Are you still awake, El?" Usually she comes in and sits on my bed and we talk, but tonight I pretend to be asleep.

She tiptoes over and is probably looking at me to be sure I'm not faking it, but I have the covers pulled up and my eyes softly closed and breathe a sigh of relief when I hear her leaving.

When the door to my parents' room shuts, I turn on my flashlight, hoping the light from it won't show under the door just in case someone decides to get up. Stuck to the present that I pull out from under my bed is a birthday card.

It's a boy's birthday card. On the front, there's a large basset hound with bloodshot eyes wearing a hunting hat, a pipe hanging out of his long mouth. Inside, it says, "Happy Birthday Champ from your drinking Pal."

Tommy has crossed out the greeting and written:
Dear Ellie or Elly or Eli (which is it),

You said you wanted a sparkly necklace and would only be getting a blue jean skirt so I found you a sparkly necklace and here it is. I hope you like it.

Love, Thomas Jefferson Bowers, the First and Last.

I unwrap the glossy pink paper and sit for a long time with the box—a shoebox from Reilly's Shoes and Bags— in my lap. My heart is beating in my mouth. I suppose I'm excited but it feels as if I'm afraid, the way my skin is sizzling and my mouth is dry.

The box, which I finally open, is full of pink tissue paper, a nest of crinkly pink, and there in the center of the nest is the largest diamond necklace I have ever seen.

At least it looks like a diamond necklace.

Diamonds aren't a big deal in my family. We only just got a dishwasher, and my mom's diamond ring, which my father gave her for their engagement, has lost its tiny diamond but she wears it anyway.

This necklace has five diamonds about the size of pennies but in the shape of teardrops, which hang from a kind of silvery chain. It's very pretty—I actually think it's beautiful—but not at all like the crazy sparkly necklace I'd seen at Wake Up Little Suzie. That one probably costs about three dollars, maybe even less, and it's made of fake sparkles. These sparkles look real.

I put the necklace on, tiptoe over to the mirror on the back of my closet door, and shine the flashlight on myself. The necklace hangs around my neck in a circle, not exactly tight but like a collar and just looking at myself, even in my pink ice cream cone pajamas, I feel older. I can hardly catch my breath.

I get a barrette from my dresser and pin my hair up so it sits on the top of my head like a powder puff. And then without even thinking about it, I take off my pajamas.

For a while, I stand in the mirror naked except for my diamond necklace, lit by a circle from the tiny flashlight. I look different, mysterious, like a girl in a movie. There are shadows around my spreading hips and light on my face and for a surprising moment, I think that I could be pretty when I get a little older.

I'm still wearing the necklace when I climb into bed. I plan to sleep in it and pull the covers up to my chin just in case Mom decides to check on me while I'm sleeping.

In the morning, I wake up to Mom calling from the kitchen that it's late, very late, and I'm going to miss Sunday school and won't get breakfast unless I hurry and already my eggs are cold. I put my hands over my ears.

But I do get up in a hurry and slip into the new blue jean skirt, which is a little tight and hard to button but it's the only skirt I have with a pocket. I drop the diamond necklace in the pocket and tie a sweater around my waist even though it's going to be hot. Lately I wear sweaters around my waist to hide my butt, but today I want it to hide the pocket bulging with diamonds. By the time I get downstairs, Milo is already crying about Sunday school. This is not unusual. Milo has a habit of crying a lot and it works. More or less he gets what he wants, which I don't remember happening when I was his age.

"My tummy's upset," he says as I rush into the kitchen, slip into my chair, and wolf down my cold eggs. Usually cold eggs drive me crazy, but today all I can think of is meeting Tommy under the Watsons' porch.

"Your stomach is often upset on Sundays before Sunday school," my father says.

"But today I think I'm going to throw up."

He scrunches down in his chair, covers his eyes with his hands, and makes little moans and hiccups.

"Don't throw up at the table," my mom says without a trace of a smile, although I know she's smiling in her head. "Ellie is trying to eat her eggs."

"Cold eggs," I say.

"You were late to breakfast," she says.

"I'm *really* sick," Milo says. "I *can't* go to Sunday school."

"No one believes you, Milo, 'cause you say it so often."

I hop up from my chair, put my dish in the dishwasher, and splash water on my face.

"Because it's *true*." Milo takes my father's hand and heads out the kitchen door to the car.

In the car, my parents decide that after they leave me at Sunday school, they'll drop Milo off at my grandmother's house so he can throw up there and then come back and meet me in time for church.

"Actually," I begin, hoping to sound sincere with that kind of casual, truthful voice that even parents who know you better than anyone might believe. "I was thinking I'd skip church and meet you afterward at home."

"Do you have plans?" my mom asks.

She must know every minute of my day. I mean, it's boring enough to live my day without having to talk about it. Besides, today I do have plans and they belong to me.

"Plans?" I say, stalling for time, and then out of nowhere, something unpleasant that I haven't even thought about for weeks hurries across my brain. *Camp.* Three weeks from today, I'll be on a train headed to Camp Farwell, Wells River, Vermont, for six weeks. Day before yesterday, I loved Camp Farwell. But now that I've met Tommy Bowers, I don't ever want to think about camp again.

"Maybe you can start to get your things together for camp while we're at church," my mom says at that very moment, knowing as she does exactly what's going on in my mind, as if she gets lost in my brain.

Just the sound of the word in my ear—"camp"—makes the blood go out of my legs and I feel weak enough to fold in half.

"I'm so glad I remembered." My mother brightens. "You'll be leaving in two weeks and we've been so busy I haven't given camp a moment's thought."

"Me neither," I say.

"So we'll pick you up at home after church is over, El," my father says, stopping the car in front of the church, telling me he'll leave a key for me under the front doormat, and off they drive, happily thinking about the weeks I'll be away at camp and it'll be just the two of them and Milo.

I walk toward the Sunday school building, watching out of the corner of my eye as our car pulls away from the curb, a little screech of tires and it heads down Miler's Road, turns right toward my grandmother's house, and disappears.

I count to fifty just in case they decide to drive around the block. Then I cross Miler's toward Pageant Street and the shopping center on my way to the Watsons' house to meet Tommy Bowers. It's almost ten o'clock. I'll probably be exactly on time, so I hope he hasn't forgotten our plan.

Usually I wear T-shirts with pants and skirts, but today I'm wearing a blouse that my mom loves because it's girly, with yellow flowers and a baby collar. I hate it because of the flowers and the stupid collar but it's the perfect camouflage for the diamond necklace, which I take out of my skirt pocket, stopping at the intersection of Pageant and Ives to fasten it. When I'm done, I slip the necklace under the collar so it's hidden, which is why I needed to wear this baby-collar blouse. It wouldn't exactly work to hide a diamond necklace under a T-shirt.

It's a beautiful, sunny day and the trees are almost in full bloom. The azaleas, mainly pink, line the front yards of the houses on Pageant Street, and all along the road the yellow tree roses that our neighborhood is famous for blow their sweet perfume into the air. I'm thinking how very happy I am.

Not that I'm usually unhappy. I used to be what my father called "Sally Sunshine" and my mother called "Our Little Cockeyed Optimist." But lately I've been feeling blue. Blue is a good word for a low-grade sadness, the way the color washes over you with its cool, slow-moving air. I've had a lot of that kind of air lately, but this morning, even with the threat of camp, I feel as if balloons are under my feet and I could take off from here and fly to the Watsons' house.

Tommy is under the Watsons' porch when I arrive. He's actually sitting in one of those striped beach chairs, which he must have brought from his house, leaning back with his arms folded behind his head. When I duck under the porch and see him there dappled in the light coming through the porch lattice, there's a sudden rush of blood through my body.

The dirt room is entirely different from how it was yesterday. There's a rug and beach chairs and a round table with a pitcher of pink lemonade and a bowl of potato chips and a beach umbrella with towels underneath it just the way it would be if we were at the ocean, except for the orange balloons. There are about ten of them, with strings of yellow ribbon, and the balloons must be filled with helium because they're hovering along the ceiling of the porch, their streamers waving.

"Wow," I say. "This is amazing."

"You're five minutes late." Tommy gets another beach chair, which he unfolds and sets next to his.

"Sit," he says.

I sit down and cross my legs, tucking my feet under my bottom. Underneath my shirt, I feel the diamond necklace cold against my skin, but I'm not going to tell him I have it on, not now. I'm waiting for the perfect time.

I notice that he has a cigarette behind his ear, and I reach over and take it, putting it between my lips.

"Light?" he asks.

I giggle. I can't help myself.

"Not just yet," I say.

Tommy has a faraway look on his face as if he's thinking about something, and then he turns to me.

"So I know what we're going to do."

"About what?" I ask. He has this way of leaving things out when he talks to me, as if we've known each other forever and I should be able to fill in the blanks.

"About here." He gestures, indicating the cave under the Watsons' porch.

"It looks beautiful. I know that," I say. And it does. A birthday party room, and it seems so strange and funny to me that a boy, any boy but particularly a boy like Tommy, the Master of Cool, would know how to make a damp, dark cave under an ordinary porch into a party room.

Tommy has taken back the cigarette, put it behind his ear.

"So now I'll tell you what's going to happen."

He picks up a plastic bag from G.C. Murphy's, which he dumps into the canvas bowl of the beach chair, and out come shaving cream and deodorant and a bag of lollipops.

"I've been shaving for over a year now in case you were wondering," he says, tearing open the bag of lollipops. "Ever since my voice changed."

"What happened to your voice?" I ask.

"Can't you tell?"

"I only heard your voice yesterday for the first time, so I don't know what it was like before."

"Different," he says.

He's walking over to the lattice door to the Watsons' porch with a bunch of lollipops, raking the ground with his foot, flattening the dirt, using his foot as a hoe. Now he's on his knees sticking the lollipops into the ground, long rows of lollipops lined up like so many flowers. When he finishes, there are four rows of lollipops about twelve inches in length, only the cellophane tops of yellow and purple and red and green lollipops showing above the ground, the sticks concealed.

"This is a lollipop garden." He stands up, brushes off his hands and the knees of his jeans. "Can you tell?"

What I want to say but it would make Tommy mad is, "Why do we want a lollipop garden?" But I don't.

"Cool," I say instead.

He folds his arms across his chest and the way he's standing makes him look older. "You don't understand what a lollipop garden is," he tells me, and he isn't smiling.

I feel suddenly weird, as if my stomach is full of soapy water and, any time now, bubbles are going to slip out from between my lips and fill the cave under the porch and I won't be able to stop them.

"So tell me what it is," I say.

He's looking at the line of lollipops, straightening the crooked ones, turning them so they all face the same way so the lines of purple and yellow and red and green are straight, and then he stands back.

"Perfect," he says. "Don't you think?"

I nod. "But I don't know what I'm supposed to be seeing."

"I told you, it's a lollipop garden," he says, exasperated.

"I see that," I say. "I just don't understand it."

"The plan is about magic," Tommy says, returning to his chair. "We're going to invite all the little kids in the neighborhood to meet us under the Watsons' porch next Saturday. We'll tell the kids they've been specially chosen for an unusual experiment in the growing of lollipops, and they'll feel so important and so lucky to know us that they won't tell their parents what goes on under the Watsons' porch."

"What does go on?" I ask Tommy.

"Magic, dumbbell," he says, looking at me strangely, as if I'm turning into the wrong kind of girl. "Haven't you ever wanted to be a magician?"

"I never thought I could be," I say. It's the right thing to say.

"Of course you can be. *You* especially," he tells me, full of excitement, his arms moving as he speaks.

I'm thinking Tommy Bowers is a strange boy and I've never met anyone like him. Some kind of mixture of *bad boy* and grown man my father's age. Just when I think I have him figured out, he ages to this other serious personality. So I need to be careful or he'll bolt from this new friendship of ours.

"This is how it will happen," he's saying, as if I'm in first grade and haven't learned to read. "The first time the kids come, we'll give them seeds, and the next week when they come, the seeds will have grown into lollipops. Very simple magic."

"Lollipops with cellophane and sticks?"

"Kids *want* to believe, so they'll believe us. I understand kids."

"Well, I don't. So what happens next?"

"Then we'll be like parents," Tommy says. "Don't you get it? They'll think we're magic like parents are and all the kids will believe us, and on Saturdays when they meet us under the Watsons' porch, they'll be our family."

"I already have a family," I say too quickly. Much too quickly.

Tommy's face turns flat, a look I haven't seen on him before, as if he's all one color and the color is snow white.

"Well, I don't have a family," he says to me. "So I'm making one."

I feel the bubbles surfacing from my stomach, coming up my esophagus, tickling the inside of my mouth, and I want them to dissolve before I explode with them.

I have let him down.

"I'm so sorry," I say. "I don't know what's the matter with me. I should have understood."

Tommy shrugs.

"It's just the truth. You don't have to be sorry."

I collapse in the beach chair next to him and he's leaning back, as he does, his arm under his head like a pillow, a look on his face as if he's thinking about something and doesn't want me to know what it is.

"So tell me how we'll make the garden," I say.

"What do you want to know?" he asks.

"Everything," I say.

And he tells me.

The plan is that each Saturday we distribute six or so seeds to every child—like zucchini seeds or pumpkin seeds or carrots—my mother has some packets of seeds in her potting shed. The kids will push the seeds into the ground in little rows and then we'll serve lemonade and cookies and tell stories and maybe play some games and then they'll go back to their own houses until the next Saturday.

In the meantime, Tommy will buy bags of lollipops and on Saturday mornings we will plant them where the zucchini and pumpkin and carrot seeds have been.

I lean back in my beach chair under the porch and watch Tommy taking the lollipops out of the ground, putting them back in the bag, tossing me one, sticking one in his own mouth, and I'm just watching him. I like watching him.

Above us, I hear the sound of someone walking, a *click . . . click . . . click*, so it must be one of the

Watson sisters and she's walking very slowly. I put my finger to my mouth to warn Tommy and he stops collecting the rows of lollipops and looks up at the floorboards. There are spaces between the boards and if one of the Miss Watsons were agile, which neither is, she could lean down and, with the sun behind her, she could see us under her porch. We stay very still and wait. Especially Tommy. I hide my face in my knees because I can't help laughing. He's assumed a pose of one of those human statues you see in shopping malls— standing on one foot, the other off the ground and straight behind him like a dancer's, his arms stretched forward as if he's carrying a tray, his expression one of mock horror.

But in time, not even very long, a door opens above us and then voices and the *click . . . click . . . click* and silence.

Tommy sits back down on the beach chair next to me.

"What're we going to do now?" I ask.

"Figure out how to get the kids to agree to come next Saturday," Tommy says.

He takes his sunglasses out of his pocket, cleans them with his T-shirt, and puts them on, as if there were any danger of too much sun under the porch.

"So," he says, looking over at me with sleepy eyes, half closed, "did you get my present or not?"

I reach down under my yellow flowered blouse and pull out the diamond necklace.

"They're real diamonds," he says.

"I know," I say.

"I couldn't find the necklace you mentioned but I saw this one in a jewelry store downtown and I just got it."

"You bought it by yourself?"

"Of course I bought it myself." He gave me a funny look. "I wasn't exactly going to send Clarissa to get it," he says. "I walked downtown and went along High Street and came to this jewelry store. The necklace was in the window, so I went in, checked out if it was real diamonds, and when the man said it was, I bought it. I told the guy at the shop it was for my mother."

"It's very amazing," I say softly.

He's quiet for a moment but I can tell he's pleased, and then he crosses his legs, stuffs his hands in his pockets, and says without looking at me, "I'm glad you like it."

Under the Watsons' porch, it's airless and silent. I look down, embarrassed to look at him, and he stares through the tiny spaces of lattice at the grass beyond and neither one of us can think of anything to say, but I'm more comfortable not talking. Even though I want to tell him how sorry I am that he's never had a real family, how sorry I am that I misunderstood why he wanted to invent a magic place for kids to come to when all I want to do is hang out here under the Watsons' porch with him. But I'm thinking how lonely it must have been all of his life, never to have a safe house, and since that's all I've ever had, I don't know what it would be like without my home. But I don't say anything because nothing I can think of saying seems to be enough.

Finally he gets up, folds his chair and I fold mine, and we lean them against the wall of the house.

"You give me a list of the kids, and today while you're having lunch at your grandmother's, maybe I'll go around the neighborhood and let the younger kids know about the lollipop garden."

"What are you going to tell them?"

"I'm not exactly sure what I'll say," Tommy says. "I'll figure a way to get them to come next Saturday morning."

He follows me out into the sunlight and we walk down the Watsons' driveway and turn right toward Tommy's house and mine.

The Brittle twins are sitting on the bottom step of their house kicking the dirt with their feet as we pass.

"Hey, guys," Tommy says.

"Hi," they say, moving the bill of their baseball caps

backward so they can better see us. "Are you Ellie's friend?"

I have a sudden sinking feeling in my stomach and want to warn Tommy that the Brittle twins may not be friendly to him, that their parents are snakes with poison in their mouths, but I don't have time to say anything.

"Ellie and I are going to be having a party next Saturday at ten o'clock in the morning and we'd like you guys to come."

"What kind of party?" Alexander asks. "Birthday?"

"Nope," Tommy says. "Magic party."

"I love magic parties," Anthony says.

"You've never been to a magic party," Alexander says.

"Well, you're invited to one now. There," Tommy points to the Watsons' house. "You turn up the driveway and walk to the end and walk under the Watsons' porch and there we'll be."

"How come?" Anthony asks.

"We're there because we're getting ready for the magic party," Tommy says.

"Dumbbell," Alexander says to his brother.

"Tell your friends," Tommy says, and we move down the street. "Tell all your friends on the block. Everyone under ten. It's an *under ten* magic party."

It's almost one and I'm expecting my parents to come home from church any minute.

"Will I see you later?" I ask.

"I don't know about tonight," Tommy says. "Clarissa has plans for us."

I can tell he has something more to say, so I ask him to call me from his bedroom when he gets back from his plans. I'll be waiting on the sunporch tonight.

"Ellie?"

"Yes?"

"I don't want you to take off the necklace I gave you."

"Okay." My voice sounds tentative.

He reaches over and buttons the top button of my blouse so the necklace doesn't show.

"And keep it hidden," he says.

We walk down the street, our shoulders touching, and as we pass his house, he pauses before running up the steps.

"So I'll see you later."

"Yes," I say. Yes, yes, yes, yes, yes!

5. Complications

I'm sitting on our porch railing so I'll be able to see my parents' car when it turns the corner into our street, and thinking about the dilemma of Camp Farwell, where I'm signed up like I was last summer and the summer before that for six weeks in the Green Mountains of Vermont.

Now that Tommy Bowers has arrived to cheer up my summer, I don't want to go anywhere for a single day, including a vacation with my parents, maybe to the beach. I actually didn't really want to go before Tommy arrived but I had rationalized that it would be okay since summer is boring at home. I'm not in the center of things in the sixth grade, and although I have friends, none of them live in my neighborhood, and P.J., probably my closest friend at the moment, goes to camp in Franconia Notch, New Hampshire, for the whole summer.

So in January when my parents asked me did I want to go back to Camp Farwell, I told them maybe, probably, yes, I did. And now I've changed my mind.

Camp isn't cheap and my parents aren't rich, so it isn't going to be easy to get out of going two weeks before camp begins but maybe I can. If I do skip, my parents will have enough money for a trip to the beach, just the two of them, leaving Milo at my grandmother's house and me home alone to fend for myself.

At this moment on a perfect June day, a circle of heat from the sun warming my arms and legs, I feel sick at heart when I think of swimming in the cold, cold lake of Camp Farwell and arts and crafts and tennis and standing at the baseline practicing my serve and horseback riding and the theater revue done every summer for the parents on visiting day. We have very few real adventures at Camp Farwell. There are two very chaperoned visits to the boys' camp on the other side of the lake and two visits to Newbury, Vermont, for a baked-bean supper at the Congregational church, and that's it for entertainment except talking after lights out to the girls in the bunks on either side of me.

And I could be spending my summer planting lollipops with Tommy Bowers.

Our blue Toyota has just turned the corner and I can see from the porch railing that only my father is in the car. Which must mean that my mother is at my grandmother's house with Milo. Not a bad time for me to bring up the problem with camp. Luckily I haven't had a chance to think about what I'm going to say to my father before I say it.

My father is easier on me than my mother is. He doesn't understand me as well as she does and so he believes exactly what I say, never imagining that I could be making anything up. My mom knows better.

When I say to him that I'm worried about money, especially since I'll eventually be going to college, and am thinking of getting a summer job, he believes me.

"What about camp?" he asks. "You can't do both."

"I love camp, Dad," I say in a sweet, singsongy voice, not too sweet but appealing, the way a daughter can be appealing to an innocent father like mine. "But I'm *twelve* and in six more years I'll be going to college and you and Mom will have to save up a lot of money in order to pay for four years of college, so I've been thinking that maybe it would be a good idea for me to start helping out. It would make me feel . . ." I give some thought to how I should phrase this, pause to consider so my father will know I'm sincere. "I think earning money for the future would make me feel grown-up."

"You're very young for a summer job, El."

"Not so young," I say. "Lots of the kids in the sixth grade have jobs."

"At twelve?"

"You know, babysitting or working at day camp or on the playground helping out the recreational program. And Darcelle Martin is even selling vegetables and fruit at her mother's stand downtown."

"That's a very responsible idea, Eleanor," my father says, and I can tell he is thinking about it, wondering whether he should support me in my plan. "Maybe we should bring it up with your mother."

"But later. Not when we're at Puss's house," I say.

My grandmother—we call her Puss—usually limits conversation to talk about her arthritis and her stomach problems and her new teeth, but she is also very quick to help us out. If my father were to say, "Ellie is thinking of getting a job to help out with the money," my grandmother would say, "No problem," and give us the money so I wouldn't have to sacrifice my opportunity to go to camp.

So this situation with camp is very delicate. I need to control the conversation as well as I can. So far I'm doing very well with my father. I can tell he's impressed that I *want* a summer job, which I certainly don't, and that he'll make an effort to persuade my mother and Puss that this plan is better than going to camp, more enriching. He likes that word "enriching."

"I don't know how your mother will feel, however," he says as we pull into my grandmother's driveway.

"She'll probably like the idea," I say, nonchalant, but I know better. My mother loves camp. She thinks it's good for me especially to be out of the way of boys and shopping malls because it was good for her and it *was* good for me but not forever.

I open the car door, but before I get out and we go into the house, I ask my father to be discreet.

"I hope Mom'll like the idea but I don't want Puss involved in any of my decisions because she gets *so* involved."

My father doesn't disagree. Puss drives him a little crazy, too.

When my grandfather was alive, I used to like coming

to Sunday dinner, not only because he was funny but mainly because Puss was so busy taking care of him, worrying over his eating and drinking and spilling and coughing, that she forgot to run our lives. Especially mine. She feels she has a right to interfere because on Tuesdays and Thursdays during the school year, when my parents are taking refresher courses at the university at night, she takes care of Milo and me and sometimes we even spend the night. And now that it's just Puss living by herself, she has too much time to develop opinions about how we should run our lives.

At my grandmother's, we usually hang around the kitchen and sometimes play cards and Puss asks about our weekend and tells us about any developments with stomach problems and my mother does her nails. She always does her nails on Sundays in my grandmother's kitchen. And this Sunday, she decides to do mine, too, so by the time lunch is ready, I have Lavender Delight on my short, stubby nails, which I bite. It's cozy, my mother painting my nails and blah, blah, blahing with Puss about work and her dance class and my good report card and Milo's poison ivy. I'm guessing that she'll be glad to have me around all summer, agreeable about my ditching camp this year, maybe even happy about it.

I'm thinking about my chances of getting a job as we sit down to lunch, Puss at the end of the table, my mother bringing the plates in from the kitchen, Milo making faces at his reflection in the mirror. All very formal and stiff.

My mother is fair and warmhearted and usually she listens, especially to kids. But of course it's her job to listen to kids. And even though she's fair about most things, she has a way of seeing through me, so she knows what I'm thinking before I even think it.

And she always knows if I'm lying, which is very inconvenient.

All during lunch, which is the same every Sunday—roast lamb and green beans and mashed potatoes and gravy and salad and ice cream cake, usually chocolate—I sit quietly eating and think about jobs.

I can't just stay home all summer and hang out with Tommy although that would be my first choice. *Hanging out*, according to my mother, is a waste of my *valuable time*. She mentions "valuable time" a lot, almost as often as my father uses "enriching."

But I'm thinking if I had a job, not babysitting but something like junior day camp counselor, my mother might decide a good job, like that, will lead to something in the future for me. She's very interested in my future. I'm only in the sixth grade and she's always saying, "That will look good on your record" or "Playing sports will help you get into college" or even more amusing, she will say, "This might help in case you decide to be a doctor or a lawyer or a professor." Everything leads to something else in my mother's world. I love her but she just can't help herself.

My father waits until we're in the car on the way home from my grandmother's house to bring up the subject of camp. Milo is sleeping in the backseat and I've pressed myself between my parents' bucket seats hoping to take charge of the conversation before my mother has anything negative to say.

"I've been talking to Ellie," my father begins with a kind of quiet formality, "and she has told me that she might want to get a job this summer."

My mother is silent.

"She's been thinking that it might be a good idea for her to begin earning her own money. Right, Ellie?"

"She's twelve."

My mother folds her arms across her chest and looks at me, speaking as if I'm not in the car.

"Eleanor is going to camp," she says.

Eleanor is my name but my mother only calls me that when she's unhappy with me, so I can tell that the nail polish moment in Puss's kitchen isn't going to last.

"We've made a down payment," she says.

"That, of course, is true." My father is trying but he's not very successful at persuasion, particularly with my mother.

"Is this your idea, Eleanor?" My mother turns so she's half over the backseat, facing me.

I've sunk into the seat next to Milo, as far away from my parents as I can get since the conclusion of this conversation is already clear.

"Well," I say, drawing my knees under my chin, my arms wrapped around my legs, "I was thinking I could begin earning some money for college and help you guys out with tuition, and anyway, even though I love camp and stuff, this would be my third year and I've already done everything there is to do at Farwell three times over."

I know, even before I finish this long sentence, that I've failed. My mother, as usual, has seen straight through my brain to the truth.

"What you really want to do, Eleanor, is spend the summer with Tommy Bowers. Child labor has nothing to do with your decision." She rolls down the window so the air blows my hair up.

"And that is something you won't be doing," she adds.

"Meg." My father is always saying "Meg," which is my mother's name, as if "Meg" translates in his mind to "no" or "please" or "hush."

"Ellie was twelve yesterday."

"Exactly," my mother says. "Too young to make her own plans."

When we turn the corner at the Watsons' house and pull up in front of our house, a police car with its lights flashing is parked in front of the Bowerses' but no one is in the car.

"Oh great," my mother says. "Do you see them?"

"Hard to miss them," my father says.

I say nothing.

If my mom makes up her mind about something, like she has done about Tommy, there's nothing anyone can do to change it.

"I can feel trouble," she says, opening the car door, taking Milo's hand, heading up our front steps.

"Don't leap too quickly to a conclusion, Meg," my father says, stopping to check out the scene on the Bowerses' front porch.

I stop, too. Clarissa Bowers is talking with two policemen. She's wearing white jeans and a red shirt and her hair is in a long braid, so she looks much younger than forty-nine, which is how old she's supposed to be. Mr. Bowers—I don't know his first name—is there, too, his arm resting on Tommy's shoulder. They are almost the same height, with the same color hair and long legs and thin hands. They look like they could actually be father and son.

When Tommy sees me walk up the steps to my house, he gives me a thumbs-up, which my mother notices, narrowing her eyes at me. She's never spanked me or raised her voice but she often narrows her eyes at me and she used to give me hard little pinches, which I hated. Her eyes remind me of those pinches.

"I'm beginning to feel so sorry for Tommy Bowers because of the way you treat him, and if it keeps up, I'll pack my clothes and move into the Bowerses' house."

This is what I say to my mother even before our front door shuts.

"You'd really move next door?" Milo asks.

"Of course I would," I say, heading for the kitchen.

"I don't want you to move, Ellie," Milo says sadly, slipping into a chair at the kitchen table, putting his head down in his arms.

I sit down beside him and whisper in his ear.

"Oh, Milo," I say, wiping the warm tears away from his

eyes. "I'd never move away from you without your permission."

Mom walks into the kitchen, puts the bag with leftover Sunday dinner on the table, and before she answers the ringing telephone, she announces a family meeting. She has what Puss would call "a bee in her bonnet," but the way she's rushing around making tea while she talks to my grandmother on the telephone, putting cookies on a plate, and telling Milo to go in the study and turn on the television, which we're never allowed to watch in the afternoon, the bee is more like a bee*hive*.

So Milo goes off to the study and I sit at the kitchen table as instructed and take a few cookies and rest my chin in my hand, waiting for disaster.

My father is reading the morning paper, keeping the paper up so it covers his face, removing himself from the conversation. But this won't last long.

I know without waiting for my mother to sit down to begin the family meeting that the subject will be Tommy and me. I'm conscious of assuming an expression of absolute boredom so I won't react with panic or fury or tears or whatever might burst out of me by accident when my mother speaks.

"Ellie." My mother's voice is soft but determined, a

practiced softness not to upset me, not to turn me against the conversation. I've heard this voice before, many times. She reaches over and brushes the newspaper so my father will put it down. Which he does, reluctantly, still reading the sports page.

"Today after we let you out at Sunday school and before church, we stopped by Lillian's Coffee Shop for croissants and there were the Links. Remember the Links?"

I say nothing, closing my eyes just slightly so I can see less of my mother than is sitting across from me. I do remember the Links. They used to live next door on the other side and Mrs. Link wouldn't let us come into her house without taking off our shoes, so I'm not interested in what the Links have to say.

"I remember them very well. Mrs. Link is a freak and Mr. Link is a wuss and I never want to see them again in my life," I say, pleased with myself.

"There's no reason for you to see the Links, but your father and I were very upset to learn from them about Tommy Bowers's reputation before he moved to this neighborhood."

"Three days ago," I say quietly. "He moved here Thursday."

"But the Links live in Cherry Hills now, where the

Bowerses used to live, and they—the Links—knew Tommy and said in Cherry Hills he was in trouble with the police."

My mother gives me a significant look.

"He was in trouble once, Meg," my father says. "They didn't make him out to be a criminal."

"The Links didn't say once. They said *in trouble*. It could have been several times but that's not the point."

When my mother is on a tear, she seems to listen very carefully to everyone but to hear nothing except her own voice. For the longest time, I used to think that she was the perfect mother, better than any mother I know. And I do still think she's better than any mother. But she does drive me crazy. Almost every day lately, she says something to me that makes me want to move to Paris for good. Recently all of the girls I know well enough to have confessions with say that their mothers are suddenly driving them crazy, too. So it must be an epidemic.

My father has folded his arms and is leaning on the table with a sense of purpose.

My mother has a tendency to push my father around, to take over the conversation, to run the house and me and Milo and even my father. But he has his own winning recipe for being a father. If he really disagrees with her, if he thinks she has gone too far or been too strict or too particular, he folds his arms across his chest and says, "Meg." And she invariably backs off.

So I'm hoping he's going to help me out if my mother has decided that Tommy Bowers is a juvenile delinquent, because already, in only thirty-six hours, Tommy's becoming my best friend.

"So what are you trying to tell Ellie?" my father asks nicely, no hostile aggression in his voice.

"I want Eleanor to be careful," my mother says. "I think Tommy may be more than she can handle."

"I will be careful," I say with great seriousness. It seems the right thing to say although I have no idea why I need to be careful.

"And what about camp?" my father asks.

My mother turns her head away, looking out the picture window in the dining room, which overlooks her beautiful garden.

"Camp." She shakes her head. "We'll think about camp, Eleanor. Later." She starts to get up from her chair, looks at me for a moment as if she's assessing my development from eleven to twelve, and then she says, "What kind of job do you have in mind for the summer?"

"I'll think about it," I say, following her lead, stuffing

the two remaining cookies in my pocket. "Are we finished with the family meeting?"

My mother nods and my father is back reading the sports page and I run up the steps to my bedroom, shut the door, head to the sunporch and get there just as Tommy has opened the window in his bedroom.

"What happened with the police?" I call in a throaty voice.

"Nothing much," Tommy says, and he seems to have no interest in the police. "So what about tomorrow? Are you free?"

"All day," I say, deciding not to tell him about camp, hoping that by tomorrow camp will be ancient history.

6. Diamonds Are Forever

I'm sitting with P.J. on my bed trying to decide whether to show her the diamond necklace, which I've slid under my bedsheets so Milo won't see it. She's come over to tell me goodbye before she goes to camp. Mainly she's been telling me about Rosie's disaster of a birthday party, but since I don't know what to tell her about Tommy Bowers and the lollipop garden and the diamond necklace, I'm having trouble concentrating on what she's saying. Something about Rosie and a 36B-cup bra.

"36B!" I say.

"36B." P.J. nods. "So, for Rosie's birthday, Lulu gave her a bra covered with daisies and matching bikini underwear and it was too small. She tried them on for us, showing off, and I thought it was totally disgusting."

We both giggle, sitting barefoot to barefoot talking.

P.J. is tall and skinny with wild black curls and pitch-black eyes and owl glasses that make her look smart, and she is. Everybody likes her. She has this amazing ability to melt into people's lives, which is something I just can't do.

"I'm a people person," P.J. says. "And you've just got attitude, Ellie, and don't want to get lost in the group. That's what I like about you."

I don't know if she's right or not. Usually I think I'm just unpopular by nature, but I'm glad that P.J. thinks it's that I don't want to be popular.

What I like about P.J. is that she's very smart about kids, especially girls, and doesn't make judgments except about Rosie. You'd have to be a god not to make judgments about Rosie O'Leary. I make a lot of judgments. Sometimes I even think of kids as either *good* or *bad*. Same goes for grown-ups. I line them up that way in one column or the other in my mind.

"The real problem is you get your feelings hurt and I don't."

"I know," I say. "I wish I didn't."

I hear my mom calling upstairs to us, "Five more minutes," before P.J.'s mom comes to pick her up.

"I *hate* that I have to go home," P.J. says. "It seems like next year before I'll see you again and on top of that I don't even want to go to camp this year."

"Me neither," I say. "It's gotten boring, don't you think? First period swimming, second period crafts, third period tennis, blah blah blah."

"Besides there're no boys for twenty miles. All girls all summer. We're too old for that."

"I know," I say, and I'm thinking I'll tell her about Tommy, just Tommy, not the diamond necklace, when she makes a kind of screech.

"There's something sharp in your bed." She's on my bed, on her hands and knees, running her hand over the sheets where she's been sitting, and of course, she finds the necklace where I've hidden it from Milo.

"What's this thing, El?" she asks, still feeling it under the sheets.

"The thing is a necklace," I say.

So I *have* to tell her how I met Tommy yesterday for the first time and I told him it was my birthday and that I couldn't have a party because of stupid Rosie and I wanted this sparkly necklace at Wake Up Little Suzie, which my parents would have thought was an impractical present, so he bought me this necklace.

"I mean he's not my *boyfriend,* P.J. He's just a friend."

She's sitting back where she was, leaning against the poster of my bed, holding the necklace up to the light.

"It's pretty," she says, turning it over in her hand, looking at it by my overhead light. "But it's not diamonds, Ellie."

"How do you know it's not?"

"They're too big. Nobody in Toledo has enough money for diamonds this big." She puts the necklace down beside her. "But it's really beautiful, El."

"I'm not telling anyone but you," I say. "Not even my parents. They'd kill me."

"How come? It was a nice thing for him to do, especially since you were having a bad day."

"My parents don't like him," I say, "because he's got a reputation."

This interests P.J. It's one of the ways we're alike.

"What kind?" she asks.

"*Bad,*" I say happily.

"Cool," she says, and we laugh and I paint her toenails with Flamingo Forever nail polish and then I hear her mother at the front door.

"So I'll write you at camp," P.J. says as she gives me one of her bear hugs, lifting me off the ground since I'm quite a bit smaller than she is. "And see you in August."

I start to tell P.J about canceling camp, but she has to leave before I can mention my job plans, because her mother is calling from downstairs in her ice-cold voice that it's time to go.

"So you better not have made a boyfriend of that Tommy guy when I come back from being with nothing but girls all summer," P.J. says. "I'd be heartbroken."

"Don't worry," I say. "He's not going to be a boyfriend, for sure."

It's nine o'clock, too early to go to bed and I'm restless. Downstairs my parents are watching *The Branhovers* on cable and Milo is spending the night at his friend Billy's house. They asked me if I wanted to watch with them but I don't want to see anything on television and I don't want to talk.

I turn off the lights, take the necklace out from under the covers, and hang it on my knee as if my knee were my neck.

Maybe it's not diamonds, I think, even though Tommy says it is. P.J. should know about diamonds even though I don't. Her family is a little rich because her father is a lawyer. And maybe Tommy made it up about the diamonds. I hope he did. I don't exactly want to go around with a diamond necklace stuck under my shirt, but I like that Tommy told me it was made of real diamonds. He wants me to believe that, whether it's true or not.

I've never felt pretty before—sort of ordinary with brown hair and freckles. But my father says I have auburn hair and my mother says I'll be a pretty woman and even *I* feel a little different about myself tonight, as if something is happening to me, some change is taking place that no one can see yet because it's happening underneath my skin.

I kiss the hard, bright teardrop diamonds one at a time.

For years my life has gone on and on, day after day very much the same as the day before. And now it's suddenly becoming another kind of life.

7. Roundup

I don't know how it happened that I fell asleep with the light on and my diamond necklace hanging on my knee but I did. When Milo comes into my bedroom, it's about seven in the morning and I'm under the covers, the necklace sleeping beside me.

"What are you doing home?" I ask Milo. "I thought you were at Billy's."

"I threw up," Milo says, climbing into bed next to me.

"I don't want you to get in bed with me if you're sick."

"I'm not sick," Milo says. "I *was* sick and Mommy came

over to get me and I got home about eleven o'clock last night."

"So you should be sleeping," I say, getting out of bed, making the bed quickly with the necklace under the covers so Milo won't see it.

"Someone woke me up. I heard a noise on the front porch and so I got up and went down and there was Tommy Bowers and now he's in the kitchen waiting to see you."

Milo goes out to the sunporch and I follow him, my heart jumping in my chest.

"It's seven in the morning," I say as if I'm very upset by Tommy's early appearance at my house. Which I'm not.

Milo flops down on one of the cots we keep on the sunporch.

"I want to have a sleepover on your sunporch. I think I'll ask Mom if I can invite all my friends this Saturday."

"You might throw up," I say, hoping my parents didn't hear Tommy come in.

"I only throw up at other people's houses," Milo says, doing a backward somersault on the cot, following me back into my room.

I'm getting dressed in a hurry without a shower, throwing my clothes on the floor because I don't have time to look through my drawers neatly for exactly what I want to wear, which are my yellow shorts. For some reason my yellow shorts are the only ones I own that don't make me look like a pear, round at the bottom. I dump out the drawer, find the shorts and a purple T-shirt that has glittery high-heeled shoes on the back and "Ellie" in silver on the front, and hand-me-down sandals from my cousin Bin.

"How come those silvery shoes are on the back of your T-shirt?" Milo asks. He's only six but very interested in fashion, especially mine.

"I like them there," I say as I brush my hair, putting it up in a ponytail.

"You look good," Milo says, "only I don't like your hair in a ponytail."

"Maybe I'll cut it off tomorrow in a feather cut like Mom's," I say, taking my hair out of the ponytail, thinking maybe it does look better down. "So, Milo, remember to tell Mom and Dad when they get up that I'm going over to the Brittles' house about a job."

"Babysitting those stupid twins?" Milo asks.

"I'd *never* babysit the stupid twins," I promise.

Milo doesn't like Alexander and Anthony for good reason. They're mean to him, double mean to him, which is the trouble with twins.

"Maybe you're going to have a job this summer and stay home?" Milo asks, hopping off my bed, following me out of my bedroom.

"Maybe," I say.

"I hope so," Milo says. "It's lonely when you go to camp and Mom and Dad want me to tell them about my day at soccer or swimming and I have nothing to say unless I made a goal in soccer."

"I know," I say. "That's why I'm trying to stay home. For you."

Milo smiles. He's a funny boy, a little whiney but easy to please and I like to make him happy.

Tommy is standing in front of the fridge, the door open, looking for something to eat.

"Hi," I say. "Do you always get up this early?"

He takes out a yogurt, finds a spoon in the drawer, and takes off the top of the carton as if he lives here—and this is only the second time he's been in my house. "Is this okay?"

"Sure," I say. It's as if he lives here.

"We've got to get started rounding up our kids if we're going to be ready by Saturday."

He finishes the yogurt, tosses the carton in the trash,

rinses the spoon, and we leave by the back door into the garden, through the gate, and into his yard.

"Maybe you'd like to see my room?" he asks.

I shake my head. "Your parents are probably sleeping."

He shrugs. "They're not my parents."

"Well," I say, not knowing exactly how to respond, "they're parents."

I walk up the street toward the Watsons' house keeping step with Tommy, our arms touching, which makes me feel a little dizzy and weak.

I've never known anyone like Tommy Bowers and I don't really understand his life of changing mothers or no parents or a bad reputation or trouble with the police. I don't even know if the things he says or the things I hear about him are true.

I think a lot about the truth since I have this tendency to tell lies. I know how complicated the truth can be, how wavering and unpredictable. I suppose I think that Tommy lies, too, that he lies even more boldly than I do since my lies are mostly inventing stories. But somehow I think I understand him even though I've only known him for two days. And I trust him, too, although any normal person would say I'm crazy.

"I had a real mother once," he says, "and then a fake

one, so I thought I was going to like Clarissa Bowers a lot. But maybe I don't."

We're walking up the street past the Brittles' house where we can see the Brittle twins in the window of the second floor. One of them is hitting the other and the other is screaming—I can't tell which but we can certainly hear "M-m-moooooom" sailing out the bedroom window over the neighborhood.

"I've already asked them to be part of the Lollipop Garden," Tommy says.

"They're my least favorite boys in the world," I say, following him up the Watsons' driveway.

"That's okay," Tommy says. "They might get better with us."

"Unlikely," I say.

I notice one of the Miss Watsons sitting in the window as we walk past and wave at her.

"That's one of them," I say. "Do you think she saw us?"

"Not a chance," Tommy says. "She's too old to see."

My mother tells me that both of the Watsons are very old and deaf and ought to have a full-time nurse taking care of them so they don't fall down the steps or burn up the house. My mom has these opinions about other people just like Puss.

Nevertheless, I doubt that the Miss Watson in the window will ever know we're running an entire camp of serious magic under her porch.

"We were robbed yesterday," Tommy is saying as we duck under the porch.

"Is that why the police were there?" I ask.

"More or less."

"What got taken?"

"Just some stuff, nothing valuable, but Clarissa was hysterical and had to take pills to calm down." He sets up the chairs for us and I sit down across from him. "Which is why I'm having my doubts about Clarissa."

He reaches over and hands me a cigarette, which I put between my index and middle finger as I've seen done in old movies, and we sit for a while without talking, the sun rising over the lattice, light dimpling our faces, a light wind rustling the trees. I'm not as uncomfortable with this silence as I might be with anyone else I can think of except my parents. Even P.J. We're both just sitting here thinking and Tommy pulls my chair closer to his so he can rest his legs in my lap.

"What are your thoughts for the lollipop garden?" he asks.

I tell him about camp, about asking my parents if I can get a job and forget sleepaway camp this summer.

"Camp would be a bummer," Tommy says. "And besides, you can't go now when I've just moved in."

"This is my idea," I say, not knowing exactly what to do with Tommy's legs, which are stretched across my lap like Milo sometimes does with me except that Milo's legs are small and Tommy's are heavy. "We invite the kids to meet us under the porch just like you said. Give them seeds, buy the lollipops, that sort of stuff. And then we have some games and tell them stories."

"So it's a day camp."

"Exactly. And I'll tell my parents that's my job. I'll say I run a little day camp on Saturday mornings for the kids in the neighborhood."

"What about me?"

"What do you mean?"

"You have a job and I don't exist. Is that the deal?"

I don't know what to say. "Well, your parents aren't making you go to camp."

"So this is just the *story* we tell your parents."

"*I* tell my parents."

"And you don't have the guts to say you're doing this camp with me?" Tommy asks, an unlit cigarette between his fingers now, his hand resting casually on the beach chair. In the filtered light, a long charcoal shadow falling across his face, he looks like someone I've seen on television, someone famous. "Your parents are worried about the trouble I've been in. That's what Clarissa tells me."

I don't respond. The truth is I don't plan to let my mother know I'm doing anything with Tommy because she'll pack my suitcase, fill the ice chest with sandwiches and juices, enough to last twelve hours without stopping, and drive me to Camp Farwell immediately.

"By the time my parents find out what's really going on, it will be too late for me to go to Vermont," I say.

"And by then, we'll be famous magicians."

I am beginning to feel that if I stay around Tommy long enough, I'll believe everything he says is possible.

There's a commotion outside, a lot of noise coming up the driveway, which I think I recognize as Brittle sounds. And then Alexander Brittle screaming *"Help!"* flies past the opening to the cave under the porch and after him Anthony Brittle.

Tommy jumps up from the beach chair.

"Guys," he calls. "Look here. I have something to tell you."

The Brittle twins come to a complete stop, turn around, and walk toward where we're standing.

"You're on private property," Tommy says.

"This is the Watsons'." Alexander leans on Anthony's shoulder. "We're allowed anytime we want."

"It's the Watsons' house," Tommy says. "But this room under the house is ours."

"Who're you?" Alexander asks.

"Thomas Bowers," he says, shaking his hair off his forehead, his hands in his pockets. "I just moved in next door to Eleanor Tremont."

"Ellie," Anthony says. "We know. Our mom told us."

"So can we come in?" Alexander asks.

"For just a minute, but you can't fight in here," Tommy says.

The Brittle twins are fireplugs with bright red, sticky-out hair, little round faces sprinkled with freckles, short legs, and long, plump bodies. Milo says they're bullies and he's probably right, but they're scared now as they slip through the opening under the porch.

"What *is* this place?" Alexander asks.

"This place is secret. It's unknown to grown-ups and kids, so you have to promise us, cross your heart and hope to die, that you will tell no one, especially grown-ups, now or ever, so help you, God."

"I don't understand," Anthony says.

"You have to understand," Tommy says quietly, leaning down to Alexander's size. "This is a secret."

"We won't tell *anyone*," Alexander says. "Not even our mother."

"Why won't we?" Anthony asks.

"Because I said so."

Anthony bops Alexander on the head.

"Do you want to know the secret?" Tommy asks.

"Yeah," Alexander says.

"Not me," Anthony says.

"Yes, you do, stupid," Alexander says.

"Yes, I do," Anthony says.

"You can grow lollipops here," Tommy says, his eyes dancing. I can hardly keep from giggling. "It's amazing. I did it myself this week."

"What did you do?" Alexander asks.

"I took fourteen seeds, planted them in the ground right here, and the next week, which was yesterday, there were fourteen lollipops."

"What color?" Anthony asks.

"Don't be stupid." Alexander turns toward his brother and gives his upper arm a push, not enough to hurt him but enough to make him lose his balance.

"I very much hate you, Alexander," he says, sulking off in the other direction.

"Ditto," Alexander says, pleased with himself.

But we can tell the Brittle twins are hooked.

Tommy sits down in the beach chair and Alexander follows him, leans against the column that goes from the porch above us into the ground, his head tilted.

"So this is a garden where you grow the candy, right?" Alexander asks.

"That's right," Tommy says. "We tested the soil and found out it has certain properties that make it possible for seeds to flourish and turn into lollipops. So that's what we're planning to do."

"And you're getting more furniture for under here?" Anthony asks.

"Furniture, yes. We're getting some furniture."

In a way I wished Tommy were telling the truth. He could tell them some of the truth and then there wouldn't be so much made-up stuff to remember. But I've already decided I'll follow Tommy to the ends of the earth or El Dorado, the City of Eternal Dreams, or to Disneyland. That's what my father says to my mother even now. "Oh, Meg," he'll say, especially when they've just had a fight, "I'll follow you to the ends of the earth or El Dorado, the City of Eternal Dreams, or even to Disneyland." And we all laugh, even my mother.

"So this is kind of a clubhouse," Alexander says.

"That's exactly what it is," Tommy says. "A clubhouse for the kids in the neighborhood."

"I'll join," Alexander says. "I'll be here next Saturday just when you said."

"At ten o'clock," Anthony says.

"And bring your friends," Tommy says.

"Which friends?" Alexander asks.

"The ones you like and trust."

"You mean my best friends?"

"All the kids in the neighborhood. Bring them all," Tommy says.

Tommy stands at the door watching the Brittle twins racewalk down the driveway making little jumps of pleasure in the air, and he turns to me, lifting his fist in victory.

"We did it," he says. "We're on our way."

8. The Sunporch

It's Monday afternoon and Milo has started swim lessons and I think my parents have left to clean up their classrooms for summer, packing away the books and student papers and costumes in the theater closet at my mother's school.

Tommy and I are in the potting shed, which my mom uses for gardening, looking for seeds—zucchini or corn or squash or even flower seeds—but we can't seem to find any on the shelves.

"We can buy some at the drugstore," I say as I look through a tool case.

"We'll find some." Tommy is rummaging in the back of an old bookcase where my mother keeps her little cardboard pots, which she fills with seeds every spring and puts in the ground in summer after the seeds have sprouted. "Here's one," he says, handing me a package of zucchini seeds.

I slip it into my pocket.

"Aren't you going to open it to see what they look like?" he asks. "They could be rat poison, you know. I read about a boy served rat poison in his cereal."

"Seeds are seeds," I say, heading for the door, planning to go with Tommy into our empty house, get out the wineglasses and lemonade and chocolate chip cookies my mom made last night for a snack, and sit on the front porch with our feet on the railing.

But I'm just out the potting shed door when I hear my mom screaming *"El-ea-nor!"* and all this time I've thought she was at school with my dad packing up for summer.

El-ea-nor means bad news, so I tell Tommy I've got to go and so does he and I'll call him from the sunporch as soon as I know what's up with my annoying mother.

"My mom is *always* changing her mind," I say. "She promised she'd be at school with my dad all morning. And she's here."

"And you can't bring me in the house like an ordinary friend because your parents think I'm a criminal?" He's standing outside the potting shed, his hands in his pockets, in full view of my mother who's probably in the kitchen looking out the window at us.

"Something like that," I say.

"Tell them I'm only a petty thief," he says, and takes off, jumping over the fence.

As it turns out, only my father has gone to clean his classroom. My mother is on the telephone with Clarissa Bowers.

"Have you seen Tommy Bowers?" she asks when I burst into the kitchen.

"No," I reply. "I saw him earlier. He was headed up to the shops."

"He's headed up to the shops," my mom says to Clarissa Bowers.

Probably at this very moment while Clarissa is standing in the kitchen with the telephone in her hand saying goodbye to my mom, Tommy is walking in the back door.

"I thought you were going to school today," I say, reaching into the cookie jar.

"Well, I didn't."

"Evidently," I say.

"Why don't you have some carrots?" she says. "I've got a fresh bag of the tiny ones in the fridge."

"Because I want a cookie," I say, sitting in a chair, looking sullen I imagine. "Sullen" is my mom's favorite word for me since Christmas. That and "don't eat this, eat that." Mom is on a healthy food kick and it makes me want to eat cookies and hot dogs and ice cream for every meal.

"We need to talk about camp," she says, sitting down at the table with the bag of carrots she's recommended for me.

"When Dad gets home," I say, putting my feet up on the kitchen table, which drives her crazy.

"We'll talk now," my mother says, reaching over to push my feet off.

"What did Clarissa call about?" I ask.

"Tommy's in trouble. That's all I know." She gathers a pile of clean towels that she's just folded and heads out of the kitchen. "She sounded upset. I don't know whether she can handle a boy like Tommy."

I follow her upstairs to my room where she collapses in my flowered rocking chair with the towels in her lap.

"El," she begins, and already I know the conversation that is coming and brace myself for it. "Any plans you may have about a job this summer are kaput." She likes the word "kaput."

"I have a job already," I say.

"What job?"

"A day camp on Saturdays for the little kids around here so parents can get stuff done."

"No," my mom says, getting up with the laundry, putting it away in the linen closet. "Next year we'll talk about jobs."

"Maybe so," I say, "but this year I'm running a camp for little kids."

"There's nothing, really nothing for you to do in Toledo this summer," my mom says. "And Saturday is only one day in the week. Six more days for you to do nothing and that doesn't work."

"I won't be going to camp," I say.

It's beginning to occur to me that I am too old for my parents to make me do anything except go to school.

"I'm perfectly capable of figuring out what to do with six days a week without help," I say.

"We'll talk to your father when he gets back."

"That's very good news," I say. "Your husband, my father, agrees with me. He told me so."

She's walking down the steps now and I think I hear my father's car in the driveway, so I slip across the room to the sunporch and lie on the cot hoping to catch a glimpse of Tommy Bowers.

*   *   *

It's sunny and softly cool on the sunporch, the heat of the early summer sun warming my skin and the only sounds I hear are birds and an occasional airplane overhead or a child crying. For some reason, I can't hear the street traffic or the sound of kids racing up and down the sidewalk. Next door Miranda is playing the violin.

I press my back into the cup of the cot, watching the trees with just the slightest of wind bend toward the Bowerses' house, keeping very still so I'll hear if someone calls.

Later I'm going to ask Tommy if he's my boyfriend, if this is what a boyfriend means. Maybe on Saturday when we go to the malls outside of town where we shop for camp clothes, which I won't be needing, I'll buy him a commitment ring.

A commitment ring is silver, sometimes plain, sometimes with engraving, and a girl and boy wear matching ones on the ring finger of their right hands. It doesn't mean they're engaged. It's like an *almost* ring.

Almost is how I'm beginning to feel about Tommy. Which means today, this afternoon, June 15, on the sunporch of my house in Toledo, Ohio, he's almost the most important person in my life.

The silky feeling running across my skin isn't a crush. "Crush" is my mother's word for Big-Time Romantic Interest. I've had a lot of crushes, twelve at least, since the beginning of kindergarten when I let Rusty Fairstein kiss my fingers while we were standing in line to go outside for recess.

This is something else. I feel as if I've swallowed a space capsule and I'm launched in a flash of light, my stomach full of Day-Glo or sequins or something sparkling inside out.

At first I don't hear Tommy call my name. And then I do.

He's standing at the window of his bedroom and his voice is a whisper merging with the street sounds.

I run over to his side of the sunporch.

"I may be detained quite a while," he says.

"Detained?"

"I'm locked in my room."

"How come?"

"I'm in trouble, so Clarissa locked me in here."

"What kind of trouble?" I ask.

"I'll tell you when I see you in person."

"You have to escape," I say.

"What would you suggest?"

"I think the only thing you can do is climb out the window. I did it once when I was punished for putting my baby tooth in Milo's mouth and he swallowed it. I tied a sheet to the doorknob and shinnied down and went over to my friend P.J.'s house and called my parents to say I was moving in with P.J."

"But you didn't."

"Of course not."

He opens the window and leans out, checking the height from his bedroom to the cement driveway.

"Maybe I can do it," Tommy says.

"When will I see you then?" I ask.

But he has closed the window.

And now he's gone.

When I go downstairs, my mother is going through some family photographs to frame. My father is gone again, this time to the market with Milo.

"We're going camping in Vermont this summer," she says cheerfully, as if what I said earlier to her about camp made no difference. "Daddy and I just decided."

"Why?" The only reason they'd be coming to Vermont is to see me at camp.

"We love Vermont." She puts a picture of Puss in a

wood frame. "Did Tommy mention to you what kind of trouble he's in?"

"I didn't see him," I say.

"That's funny. I thought I heard you talking to him just a little while ago."

"That wasn't me," I say.

She has a picture of Milo and me in Vermont last summer. Milo's on a pony, I'm sitting on a fence, the sign for Camp Farwell is behind us.

I put my head down on the kitchen table, resting it on my folded arms, my face turned away, and I'm thinking that I'd like to tell her things the way I used to do when I was younger, even last year when I'd tell her everything important to me.

But now if I tell her about Tommy Bowers, I'll probably be shipped to Thailand just to keep me away from him.

She must be looking through my brain as usual because she reaches over, pulling the hair away from my face, and says, "Tell me what it is you like so much about Tommy Bowers."

"Tommy Bowers?" I act surprised, as if I have a lot of Tommys in my life.

"It's clear you like him very much."

"I do," I say. "We disagree about a lot of things lately."

"Not necessarily," she says. "I'm interested in your friendship with Tommy because you're very picky about friends and, even though I know you'd like to be popular like Rosie O'Leary, you're really too particular to be popular." She finishes putting the picture of me with Milo in the frame and sets it up on the table. "I admire that."

"Admire?" I ask.

Truthfully I'm pleased but I can tell she's trying to get in my good graces after our camp fight and I'm not ready for that. Moms have a slippery way about them. At least mine does.

Of course I want to be popular, and "particular" is just an excuse for not being popular.

"So what do you think? I've never seen you grow fond of someone new quite so quickly."

I wonder how much she knows, whether she knows that I've seen Tommy a lot or is just guessing, whether she can *tell* how much I like him.

"Why do you want to know?"

"Why do you think?" she asks.

I rest my chin on my fists and watch her working.

"You've never had a good friend who's a boy. Because he's had a hard life—I've never known a child to have a harder one and perhaps you haven't either and that's interesting to you."

"His hard life?" I ask. "I don't think so."

But that's not exactly true. I like Tommy's story. It's like a story in a book about a boy abandoned by his mother, who can't find a family, and even though he now lives with Clarissa Bowers and her husband, Mr. Bowers, he is really *alone*.

And I like that he's unafraid of trouble.

I'm quiet, knowing that part of what I like about Tommy Bowers worries my mother. He's what my grandmother Puss calls "a bad boy"—she's even said with a twinkle in her eye that when she was young, she liked "bad boys" because they were exciting. Once I asked if my father had been a "bad boy" and she said no, and when I asked what he had been like when he was young, she used words like "good" and "responsible" and "loyal" and "hardworking." And my mother, who was with us at the time, said, "He was exciting to me, Puss."

Grown-ups are weird and luckily I can't understand them.

"I suppose what I like about him is that he likes me," I say finally.

My mother smiles, fixing a picture of my father in another frame.

"That's not a very good reason, Ellie."

I don't look at her although I can tell she's looking at me, her head cocked just so, like an elderly teenager, her hair recently dyed with yellow stripes, "streaked" she calls it, and up on the top of her head in little combs.

"Sometimes I don't tell you the truth because I'm afraid you won't like to hear it," I say, which is absolutely true.

The truth is interesting. I have told a lot of harmless lies. It's a habit of mine to tell certain lies like the one about Tommy walking up to the shops, but seldom, maybe never, do I lie about the way I feel in my heart.

"So you want to know the truth?" I ask. "Tommy makes me feel important and I've never felt important, really important, except with you and Dad and sometimes Milo."

My mother says nothing. She is sorting through her pictures, putting them between the pages of an old photograph album, and I'm looking out the window of our kitchen at the potting shed and garage and garden as if it's the first time I've actually seen them.

And finally, she says in a way that is sweet and worrying at the same time, "Oh, El, I hope I can let you be friends."

I'm lying on the cot on the sunporch, talking to Rosie

O'Leary on the portable phone, when my parents leave to take Milo to a birthday party at Billy's house and then they're going to a seven o'clock movie, so that means they won't be home until about nine-thirty. Plenty of time for me to meet Tommy if he manages to get out of his bedroom. Lately my parents allow me to stay home alone if they're not going to be late, but I'm surprised they're willing to let me stay alone tonight since certainly my mom guesses I'll be with Tommy Bowers the minute I have a chance.

Unless she knows something I don't, which isn't likely.

I hear the front door shut and Milo's whiney voice. The car pulls out of the driveway and I'm still lying on the cot on the sunporch listening to Rosie babble on about Rebecca Foater and what a baby she is and how Brianna had her hair dyed because her mother thought it was mousy and how Tina Freed has a boyfriend from the junior high. Typical Rosie. She has opinions about everything and we're not even friends.

"So, El, I hear you've got a new boyfriend," she says in that *I-know-everything-about-you* voice that I hate.

"Wrong!" I say in my ice-water voice, which I've learned from my mother.

"Tina told me today when I saw her at swimming,"

Rosie says. "A new boy just moved in next door to you."

"A new boy did just move in next door but I only met him the day before yesterday. Not exactly enough time to be his girlfriend."

"I hear he's supposed to be really hot and smoke cigarettes and act kind of old for his age."

"He looks like a regular boy to me." I'm enjoying this conversation and I imagine Rosie's very sorry she didn't invite me to her birthday party. Too bad for that. I don't plan to tell her one true thing about myself for the rest of my life.

"Tina said she heard from Maida about him. His name is Tommy, right?"

"That's the name of the boy who lives next door," I say.

"Well, I was just thinking I've got nothing to do tonight and my mom could drive me over to your house and we could hang out or you could come over here if you want. There's night swimming at the pool till nine o'clock."

"I can't," I say. "I'm going to the movies."

"With who?" Rosie asks, not missing a beat. She is impossible.

"With my parents," I say.

"I could come with you and then you could sleep over at my house."

We have call-waiting on the phone and it's beeping now, so I tell Rosie goodbye, that I have to take this call because I'm expecting my grandmother, and she hangs up.

I'm very glad to hear P.J.'s voice on the other end of the phone because she's the only one who knows about Tommy Bowers, and if she's told Tina Freed or anyone else, I'm not going to write her at camp this summer.

"I told no one," she says to me when I ask. "You're my best friend. I'd never talk about you behind your back."

"Tina Freed heard it somewhere."

"Tina called me and said Maida was driving down your street with her mom and saw you standing with Tommy in front of his house. Maida called Tina who told Rosie and me and probably the whole class. I'm really sorry."

"S'okay," I say. "It's not your fault. At least it's summer and we won't be seeing everyone in the class, and by the time school starts, they'll have forgotten and Tommy will be history."

"And you'll be at camp, anyway."

"Not likely," I say. "Camp is canceled."

"Canceled?"

"By me. My mom and I had a little argument and I won."

But just at that moment, I hear Tommy calling my

name, so I tell P.J. goodbye and run to the Bowerses' side of the sunporch.

I don't notice Tommy at first although I'm looking directly at his bedroom. But it's dusk with dusty light and shadows appear to be objects and objects appear to be shadows. So when I see his head at the top of my vision, I think it's the branch of a tree. I cup my hands in the shape of binoculars so I can see in the shadows and there he is already shinnying down a line of sheets tied together at the ends.

9. Under the Watsons' Porch

I run downstairs, check the time—7:30, which means another two hours before Mom and Dad get home from the movies—grab a flashlight, and head up the street in the dark toward the Watsons' house. Even before I get there I see the flickering lights under the porch, and ducking under the eaves, I see Tommy in blue jeans and a dress shirt with the sleeves rolled up and bare feet. He is lighting votive candles he's scattered around the dirt floor.

"Hi," he says, looking up at me. "I made it out of jail."

I flop down on the beach chair.

"Did you just leave the sheets hanging out your window?"

"What else? They're tied to my bedpost and besides they only go halfway down, so I had to jump almost a story to the ground."

"Scary. I saw you from the sunporch."

"Wine?" he asks.

"Please."

The pitcher of pink lemonade is still on the table from yesterday and he pours a plastic glass for each of us. He takes a Snickers bar out of his pocket, takes off the wrapper, splits it, and gives me one half. He eats the other half standing beside my chair, his foot on the edge, sort of leaning on his knee while he talks to me.

"It's turning out that I don't like the Bowerses."

"Why?"

"He's a wimp with a big voice and a bad temper, and I used to like her but she's too nervous," he says. "The thing is, I really *want* to like living with them but it's looking sketchy." He moves a beach chair so he's facing me, very close, almost face to face, and in the flickering light from the candles he looks eerie and wild-eyed and so much older than I am. I feel suddenly shy.

"I was locked in my room because Clarissa was freaked out about the robbery," he said.

"What does that have to do with you?" I ask.

"Nothing. That's what I mean. She's a hysteric."

His hand falls across the arm of my chair, close to my hand, and I'm conscious of it there, thinking he's going to hold my hand but he doesn't.

"You've probably been wondering why I want to be with little kids," he says. "Isn't that right?"

"Kind of. Most kids our age don't."

"It's like this. When I sat all day today in my room on my bed with nothing to do, I started thinking about my life. That I've never really *belonged* to anybody. Not to Clarissa and not to the other mothers I've had, and somehow it makes sense to have these little kids belong to me even one day a week. Sort of be *my* kids."

I don't exactly know what he's saying but I nod and say I do, and he looks over at me with an expression on his face I haven't seen before. Maybe lonely or sad or unhappy.

"I don't think you do know exactly," he says in a nice way.

"But I want to understand." Which is true.

He reaches over and takes my hand then, and in a

breath of a second, he is leaning toward me and I know that he's going to try to kiss me.

"Not yet," I say, quickly pulling away, and I don't understand *why* I pull away except I'm probably afraid. Not of his bad reputation. I'm afraid because he's a boy who is going to kiss me and that's never happened to me before. Right now I think I will *die* if he does it and that's not because I don't want him to kiss me, because I do.

"More wine?" he asks, picking up his lemonade and finishing it in a single gulp.

"Yes, please," I say. "The wine is excellent."

10. Zucchini Seeds

It's Saturday morning, a week after my birthday, and I'm sitting on one of the striped beach chairs under the Watsons' porch. I'm watching Tommy, who is standing at the lattice door waiting for the kids in the neighborhood to arrive. It's almost ten o'clock and we've been here since eight-thirty.

I was a little late because of the camp problem. Milo told me about the problem last night, coming into my bedroom after my lights were out and climbing into bed next to me, folding his little arms across his chest.

He didn't wake me up. I was too excited about today to sleep.

"Are you awake?" he asked me.

"Yup," I said. "Can't you sleep?"

He shook his head, nuzzling into my side.

"Pit bulls?" I asked.

"Two of them. One is white with long teeth in the front of his mouth," he said.

"You can sleep with me since the pit bulls never come into my room and Mom and Dad have gone to bed."

"I know. I checked and they were already sleeping," Milo said. "Did they tell you about camp?"

"Nothing new," I said.

As far as I knew, the decision about camp was on hold. I had decided not to bring it up until after the first day of the Lollipop Garden, but I knew that my parents were still expecting me to go to Camp Farwell as planned since Mom came home on Friday afternoon with six pairs of new white socks and six new underpants with balloons and kittens and half moons on them, which look like the underpants of a five-year-old.

I plan to buy bikinis with my allowance the next time I go to the shopping center with P.J. She's been wearing bikinis for over a year. But I know my mom isn't in favor of changing my style of underwear and that she hasn't changed her mind about camp either, because the duffle bag I take to camp is hanging in the shower airing out.

"So this happened tonight at dinner while you were at the movies." Milo was lying on his side, resting his head in his hand, talking. "The camp person, Mr. Farwell, called and Mom said she was not absolutely sure about our plans for you to go to camp because of complications at home, and Mom said she was sorry she hadn't sent the balance in and Dad said to let him talk to Mr. Farwell and so he did and told him the money would be in by Monday and he hated to be late but I can't remember what else, something about where the money got lost."

Milo sometimes speaks in one long sentence without any periods and is out of breath before he stops speaking. But he has a very good memory for details and even remembers the exact vocabulary of what he hears, so I pay attention when he has something to say, because it's probably right.

"So you see?" he said.

"I do see," I said, although I certainly didn't.

"Maybe now you'll be home all summer with me and you can take me to Gymboree and soccer practice."

"That's true," I said. "I can do that."

And sometime not long after that, we both fell asleep in my bed.

*   *   *

My mother was already up in the kitchen reading the paper when I got up at seven this morning hoping my parents were still sleeping so I could leave a note for them.

But she was up and my father was watering the lawn, so I slipped into a chair across from her and tore the paper off the shredded wheat biscuit, put it in a bowl, and drowned it in milk.

"We spoke to Mr. Farwell last night," she said. I pretended to be surprised but not particularly interested.

"We're late to send in the balance we owe and he called to say we have to decide by Monday and he'll still keep the deposit."

"What's a deposit?" I asked.

"We sent in a check in order to hold your place in camp," she said.

My parents don't talk to me about money ever although I know we're not rich, because they're schoolteachers, and that we're not poor, because there's nothing that I need— which is different, of course, from nothing I want.

"Mmmm," I say, not wishing to "rock the boat." That's Puss's term for causing unnecessary trouble.

"So?" my mother said.

I suppose the question was addressed to me but I decided not to answer although I knew exactly what I planned to do.

I planned to say nothing about camp unless I was told point-blank that I would be going. Then I'd say, "Wrong. I won't be going." And sometime about three days before camp, when Mom asks me to pack my duffle and get toothpaste and shampoo and stuff at the drugstore, I'll tell her that camp is kaput.

I will not be going and there is no way I can be forced to go, even if she calls the police. The poor overworked police of Toledo will think she's ridiculous.

I get up from the table and put my cereal bowl in the dishwasher.

"See you later," I say.

"You're going to the camp now, right?"

"My camp," I say nicely enough.

I'm sure Mom didn't see me go into her potting shed but my father did since he was watering the lawn, so I told him I'd left my barrette in the shed. I found a packet of zucchini seeds on the middle shelf, dropped it into the pocket of my yellow cargo shorts, and headed toward the gate.

"See you later," I call to him, but he has rounded the corner of the house and can't hear me.

I'm sitting on the beach chair too nervous to look down Lincoln Road to see if anyone is coming.

"They'll be here," Tommy says.

I don't question him. He's counting on the Brittle twins to tell most of the other kids in the neighborhood although Tommy did write a note on his father's computer to every family on the block with small kids:

Come to the Lollipop Garden for Fun and Games

Saturday, June 20, at 10 a.m.

Under the Watsons' Porch

Ellie Tremont

He wrote it like an invitation and he signed my name.

"I signed your name because they don't know me," he said.

What I especially love about Tommy Bowers is that he's fearless. I like to think of myself as fearless but I'm not. I'm too much of a worrier. I like to be around trouble but I don't want to be in it myself. I didn't really know this until I met Tommy.

Now he's walking just beyond the entrance to the porch and down the driveway, looking right at Lincoln, checking for children. I can see little triangles of him in the morning sun through the lattice.

I'm heading out to join him when he runs back, ducking into the Lollipop Garden, an expression of pure happiness on his face.

"They're coming!" he says.

"How many?" I ask.

"All of them are coming. That's what it looks like."

We stand aside and they file in.

Billy Block walks in with Anthony Brittle, carrying a stuffed pig in one hand, his other hand in the pocket of his shorts. His sister Sarah comes in holding Hannah Joseph's hand. I can tell Hannah has been crying and reach down to ruffle her hair.

"My mama says I can only stay five minutes," she says to me. "And I told her I didn't know how long is five minutes and she said I better stay home then and so I cried."

"And then her mama said she could come," Sarah says.

Alexander is carrying a Wiffle ball and bat, bopping Anthony over the head from time to time.

"Everybody except Jonathan Bellman, who has a cold," Alexander says.

"He has strep," Sarah says. "Is this a camp?"

"It's a camp," Tommy says.

"Do you have horses?" Hannah asks.

"Not yet," Tommy says.

"But they will," Miranda Salon says. "I heard from Alexander that soon you'll have horses for us to ride."

"Possibly," Tommy says.

Lisa Bellman is in her nightgown. At least it looks very

much like a nightgown, with a long yellow cotton skirt and a strappy top and she isn't wearing shoes.

"There're rats under here," Sarah says to her. "You should've worn shoes."

"There're no rats under here," I say to her. "We don't allow them to come."

"How can you be sure?" Lisa asks. "It's very dark and shadowy."

"I have a lot of experience with rats and they don't like this kind of place," Tommy says. "Too musty, too much dirt. Not a rat kind of place at all."

Ian and Sean and Cara O'Shaunessey come together, sleepy-eyed from watching cartoons on television, blackberry jam from breakfast painted on their lips.

"Is this the place where we're invited?" Cara asks, peering inside.

"Yeah," Alexander says. "Can't you tell?"

I hear one more set of footsteps on the driveway and Milo walks in with his baseball cap on backward and his shorts, too, so the fly is in the back.

"So this is the clubhouse where you'll be coming on Saturday mornings." Tommy is standing at the entrance, his arms folded across his chest, his hair flopping across one eye. "Amazing things will happen."

"Like what?" Sarah Block asks, keeping close to the entrance.

"Like this," Tommy says. He pulls the door to the Lollipop Garden closed and kneels down beside the small plot of dirt in which he has dug four narrow furrows.

"See these lines in the dirt?" He speaks very softly. "Last week Ellie and I planted some seeds here that we had heard would grow into lollipops. We didn't believe it was possible but we planted them anyway." He reaches over, digs deep in the dirt, and pulls out a lavender lollipop covered in cellophane.

"And the next time we came back, this is what we discovered. Lots of them, enough to last a week. So . . ." He stands up with a funny expression on his face— "devilish" is what Puss would call it—as if it is the most normal thing in the world to be under the Watsons' porch with all the neighborhood kids growing lollipops. "So Ellie and I asked you to come to this secret place because the earth under the Watson house is magic for children. Things happen here that can't happen anyplace else in the world."

I didn't know he'd hidden a lollipop under the dirt this morning. He didn't tell me. Even for me who knows this place, this clubhouse, this garden of lollipops, there's a shiver of something like magic in the damp air.

"See?" Alexander speaks up. "What did I tell you guys?"

"Alexander told us about the lollipops," Hannah says, "but we didn't believe him."

"I did," Lisa says.

"Not me," Billy says, looking askance at Tommy.

"You shouldn't believe it until you see it with your very own eyes."

I pick up a cup belonging to Clarissa that I've filled with the zucchini seeds.

"So, guys, do you want to plant your own seeds?"

"I do," Milo says, and takes one from the cup.

"Me too," Sarah says.

Lisa and Hannah gather around me.

"How many seeds do we get?" Sean O'Shaunessey asks.

"Twenty," Ian laughs.

"Six each," Tommy says.

"I thought we'd get seven," Billy says. "One for every day of the week."

"Seven is fine," Tommy says. "Seven is the exact right number."

Miranda holds her tiny hands palm up and I count out seven seeds. And then I count out seven for Milo and Sarah and Lisa and Hannah and Alexander and Cara and Anthony and Billy and Ian and Sean.

"What about Jonathan?" Lisa asks.

"Jonathan can plants his seeds when he's here," Tommy says.

"But he can't be here today because he has strep."

"Part of the magic is that you have to plant your own seeds in order for them to grow. Ellie puts the seeds in your hand and they get to know you, lying in your hand like that, and then you plant them in the ground and they're your seeds, your very own, no one else's."

"So they grow for us especially?" Cara asks.

"That's right," Tommy says.

"Seeds aren't alive," Anthony says, looking at the little dark specks the size of fleas in his hands.

"Of course they're alive," Tommy says. "Everything, even you, starts as a seed."

"I didn't," Billy said.

"I was a dinosaur," Ian says.

"A dinosaur started as a seed," I say.

"No way," Billy says, but he's down on his knees now with the other kids, punching his seeds into the ground the way Tommy has told them to.

Hannah looks up.

"What if you drop your seeds?" she asks.

"Did you?" I ask her.

She's on her knees beside the line of furrows, her hand out, counting the number of seeds there.

"Be very careful, guys," Tommy says. "Seven seeds each but that's all you get. No more if you drop one."

Miranda looks up with a pout.

"And no crying," Tommy says. "You have a special job here and you need to rise to the occasion."

"What does that mean?" Anthony asks.

"Don't lose your seeds," Sarah replies.

The sun is sliding up the lattice toward noon and the garden is planted. We've already played Pirates and Forget-Me-Not and gone around the circle so everyone got to tell one dream and Hannah falls asleep on Sarah's shoulder.

"Next week," Tommy says. "Same time, same place."

And one by one, they duck under the porch, through the lattice door, and out into the sunshine, slipping by Tommy and me.

Miranda is the last to leave. As she passes Tommy, she takes her thumb out of her mouth and looks up at him with her wide-set olive-colored eyes.

"Are you a magician?" she asks.

"If you think so," Tommy says.

She nods. "I think you are."

11. The Sunporch

Tommy and I are on the sunporch, each lying on a cot, me on my stomach, Tommy on his back using his arm for a pillow, smoking his usual unlit cigarette. Outside it's raining, just a whisper of rain brushing the trees, soundless on the roof above us.

It's late afternoon and my parents are playing softball in their summer league at the playground, Milo is at Sean's house spending the night. Or pretending to spend the night. By midnight, he'll throw up and Ms. O'Shaunessey will call Mom and Mom will pad barefoot down Lincoln Road in her bathrobe and pick him up. I don't know why my parents keep saying yes when Milo wants to spend the night or why Milo even asks. It's always the same story.

I'm wearing my yellow cargo shorts, which are smudged from sitting in the dirt under the Watsons' house, and a T-shirt of my mom's that I gave her for Mother's Day this year with "BEST LITTLE MOM IN TOLEDO" written on the back in primary colors. When Mom washed the T-shirt, the primary colors ran into a rainbow of reds and blues and greens all over the white cotton, so I took the one I gave her and Dad bought her another.

I don't know why it makes me laugh to have a T-shirt with "BEST LITTLE MOM" on it since I'm the most unmom-like twelve-year-old in the world and don't even babysit except in an emergency. And I certainly wouldn't be doing this lollipop camp if Tommy hadn't come along with his ideas.

"Really amazing," I say.

I don't need to listen to what he says because he keeps saying the same thing. Maybe forty times, he's said it, each time ending with a question so I'll have to respond.

He's right of course. It was amazing that every single younger kid on the block came except Jonathan. That they *believed* us.

"Did you notice that they actually *believed* us?" Tommy asks.

"Of course they believed us. You were so good at persuading them."

"I was, wasn't I?"

"You were."

I don't feel the same way as Tommy does about the Lollipop Garden but I'm beginning to understand him. This morning after all the kids left and we were walking down the hill to our houses, he told me that last night trying to get to sleep he'd made believe the kids were orphans like he is and he and I had adopted them and for those two hours under the Watsons' porch, they were our kids.

"What did you think about when they left to go home to their real parents?" I ask him.

"I didn't think about it," he says.

Tommy is sitting up now, his cigarette in his pocket, and he's leaning against the wall.

"What does it mean, 'Best Little Mom in Toledo'?" he asks. "How many people have this shirt?"

"Probably a hundred," I say. "We got two of them."

"So what does it mean if there're so many best moms?"

"It's a joke," I say. "It's just that everyone thinks his mom is the best, right?"

"I don't believe everyone thinks that." His arms are folded across his chest, his lips tight.

I'm suddenly quiet.

"Are you mad at me?"

He shakes his head no and I'm planning to change the subject but he won't let me.

"So what is a best mom?" he asks. "Do you know?"

Most of my friends take their mothers for granted—mothers are mothers after all and they stick around most of the time, and by the time a kid gets to be my age, mothers drive us a little crazy.

But I've almost never thought what it would be like not to have a mother. I don't want to think about it.

"My mother's got all these rules and gets into my business all the time," I say, "but she's sort of like the fence around our yard."

"Remember you told me you still love her even though she drives you crazy?"

"I do."

"I don't think I've ever loved anyone except the mother I never knew, who's in my imagination."

I go silent, thinking I should say something but maybe Tommy just likes talking and doesn't need to hear anything back. Maybe he's never spoken about his true life before and he only wants me to listen, which I'm doing, my heart beating hard in my chest.

"Maybe I love you," he says, and I can't tell if it's a joke or truly what he's thinking. "And maybe not. Who knows?" he says with a coy smile. "Certainly not me."

The sunporch has filled with heat, blown in from somewhere underneath the porch, hotter than it's been all day although I can see the wind blowing the trees and it shouldn't be this hot, so high up in the trees. There's a sweet smell in the air, maybe the wind is lifting the scent of flowers from the garden through the screens to the sunporch. My skin feels shivery, almost transparent, too thin to contain my blood, to conceal my quivering muscles. My stomach is wild with the flapping tickly wings of butterflies. And I feel like Milo must when he goes on a sleepover, sick with excitement and fear and longing for what I don't know.

Instinctively, I reach under my shirt and pull out the diamond necklace so it rests on top of the "MOM" T-shirt.

Tommy looks bored to death.

"Very pretty diamonds, Eleanor Tremont."

"This necklace is the perfect present of my life," I say.

12. A Reality Bite

It's Tuesday and I haven't seen Tommy since Saturday on the sunporch. I lie in bed at night and watch the Bowerses' house but no one seems to be at home. My friend Linsay called to say goodbye, she's off to the mountains with her parents and could I come over and spend the night. That was Monday. I said "No, I can't" and made up an excuse.

The strangest thing has happened. I don't want to leave my house. I wouldn't go to the movies last night with my parents. I told Vera, a friend from Sunday school, that I was feeling a little sick when she asked me to go to the mall.

This morning at breakfast, my mother sat at the table with me while I ate my cereal. I didn't look up but I knew she was watching me.

"What's going on with you, Ellie?" she asked me finally.

"Nothing much."

"Something is. Maybe not much but something," she said.

I got up from the table, dumped the bowl of half-finished cereal in the sink, and put it in the dishwasher.

"I'm overtired," I said.

"Maybe it's your immune system."

Recently my mother has taken an interest in boosting the immune system of everyone she knows, something she's read about since it's the new subject of conversation with her friends.

"I don't think so but thanks for your interest," I said, heading upstairs to my bedroom. "My immune system is fine."

I don't know what has happened to Tommy and I don't want to ask my parents because I'm afraid to let them know I'm interested. He left my house on Saturday in the late afternoon and told me he was going to be busy on Sunday but would see me Monday, and then he was gone. I lay in the dark on the sunporch Sunday night waiting for the light in his bedroom to go on. But it never did. Monday I sat on the front porch after Milo left for day camp and my parents went to teach summer school, which they do for extra money in the mornings. I was drinking lemonade waiting for Tommy to run down the front steps of his house. But nothing happened all day long, and by Monday night when Linsay called me for a sleepover, I was feeling sick.

"Blue?" my father asked me that night when he came in to tell me good night.

"A little," I said.

"It's always depressing for a few days after school is out for summer vacation even though you thought you couldn't wait," he said. "You'll be glad to be at camp."

"I don't think so," I said. "I'm not planning to go."

"We'll talk about it," he said. "There's a lot to take into account."

"What does that mean?" I asked.

"It means the subject of camp isn't finished," he said.

"Maybe for you," I said, "but it's finished for me."

He didn't argue but that doesn't mean anything. He doesn't argue very often.

I'm lying on my bed looking at the ceiling thinking about

Tommy when I hear my mother come up the steps, stop by my door, hesitate, and knock.

"Yes?" I call.

She opens the door but doesn't come in. Just leans against the entrance watching me change from my pajamas to shorts.

"Do you have plans?" she asks.

"I leave for Hawaii at noon," I say without cracking a smile.

"I mean before you leave for Hawaii," she says.

I like that about my mother. It comes of spending her entire grown-up life with kids my age.

"I'm hanging out here."

"All day?"

"Probably."

"It's interesting, you know," she begins, and I can tell she's warming up to one of those long conversations she likes to have, a heart-to-heart with her daughter. "The little camp you ran on Saturday morning? I was talking to Maud O'Shaunessey at the market and she said her kids love the camp. They can hardly wait until next Saturday."

"Good." I'm checking my dresser for T-shirts although I'm no longer interested in what I wear.

"Ms. O'Shaunessey said you're having a magic camp.

What does that mean?" Mom asks. "Learning magic tricks?"

"Sort of," I say.

"Hannah's mom said that you've made a kind of clubhouse under the Watsons' porch."

I shrug. I don't know what to tell my mother but I can see she's preparing to slide into my life as usual.

I'm wondering if she knows about Tommy or if she thinks I'm doing this magic camp alone. Milo is great about keeping secrets and he knows how our parents feel about Tommy Bowers, so he'd never get me into trouble on purpose.

"Did you ask the Watson sisters if you could use the porch?" She has moved into my room, leaning now against the bookcase.

"The camp is *under* the porch," I say, and toss my sneakers back into the closet, planning to go barefoot even though it's cool today.

"Nevertheless."

"The Watson sisters are deaf. You told me that yourself."

She's careful with me but she's making no effort to leave my room, which she knows I want her to do.

"I did ask the Watson sister with the white hair if we could be under her porch on Saturday mornings," I say, which isn't exactly true. "She didn't hear me of course but she smiled, so I'm sure it's perfectly fine."

"Good for you."

She's moved over to my bed and is sitting on the end of it, her legs crossed, her hands folded. Other mothers would have bolted from the bedroom of a bad-tempered daughter by now. It's one of the difficulties of a mother who's a teacher. She's not afraid of me. P.J.'s mother is so afraid of P.J. that she hides in the laundry room pretending to do laundry until P.J. leaves for school. But I'm *nothing* compared to the juvenile delinquents in my mother's classes.

"I don't want to talk about this," I say, opening the door to the sunporch, checking the weather, which is cloudy, checking Tommy's room, which is dark.

"You don't surprise me, Ellie. But I do want to talk about it. I want to know what you're doing with the children in the neighborhood. It's *our* neighborhood and I should know when people like Maud O'Shaunessey bring it up at the grocery store."

"Ask Milo," I say, checking out Milo's loyalty to me.

"Oh, darling, we both know Milo tells us nothing personal except his tummy hurts and the pit bulls are back again. He told me camp was great. I asked him what went on. He said nothing happened. So?"

I smile in spite of myself. Good old Milo.

"It's a lot of kids," she says, and already I know what's coming. "Are you able to run this camp alone."

I don't reply. I gather some books from my bookcase as if I'm planning to spend the day reading. I take a drawing book from my desk drawer since I like to draw the insides of things, like animals and birds and even buildings— things like the heart and intestines and liver and stuff or the essential structure of a building. I don't know why. The insides of things have always interested me more than the outsides.

"Hannah Joseph told her mother that a boy was helping you. She didn't remember his name."

I turn around, my arms full of books and a drawing pad and I grab a handful of pencils from the cup on my desk.

"Everyone in the neighborhood knows his name, Mom. Especially you."

And I head downstairs, through the kitchen where Milo is having breakfast with my father, out the back door to the potting shed where I plan to spend the morning out of view.

The potting shed has a heavy smell of dirt and damp, almost a feeling of living underground. I spread out a burlap bag against the wall and sit down with my drawing pad. It's a new one, only the first two pages are filled. I did these drawings—hearts, livers, kidneys, that sort of stuff—at my grandmother's house last Sunday when I was bored as usual.

The third page has the beginning of the letter I started to Tommy.

I want to tell the truth in this letter but I don't know how to say it. I don't even know whether I'll see him again. He seems to be the kind of person who disappears or his life disappears and he has to find a new one.

Perhaps Clarissa and Mr. Bowers have decided Tommy is too much trouble. Or changed their minds and want a baby instead of a boy. His life with the Bowerses seems temporary. Nevertheless, I don't understand why, if he's left forever, he didn't bother to tell me goodbye.

I hear the slapping of feet and Milo bursts into the potting shed.

"There you are," he says. "I thought you were lost."

"I'm hiding out from Mom."

"She said you hate her."

"I don't hate her," I say. "I wish she'd leave me alone. She's always in my business."

"She wanted to know whether you were running the

camp by yourself and so she asked me if anyone was helping and I said no one was helping you because you're
helping Tommy, isn't that true?"

"More or less. But thank you, Milo. You're a very great
brother."

"But Mom said isn't it true that Tommy Bowers was
there, too."

"And you said yes?" I know Milo and he's not like me.
He tells the truth, and if he doesn't, if he tries to make up
a story, he's a terrible liar, so he may as well tell the truth.

He nods.

"That's okay, Milo. You had to tell her."

"You're not mad?"

"Not at all," I say, and I'm not. "If she wants to go bal-
listic about Tommy Bowers, that's her problem. He's my
friend."

"Me too," Milo says happily. "He's my friend, too."

And he dashes out the door and up the back steps, on
his way to day camp with my father.

What I like best about you . . . I begin a list of the
things I like about Tommy.

1. You make magical things happen.

2. You make me happy and sunny.

3. You think about other people instead of yourself.

4. *You are almost always in a good mood.*

5. *You don't complain.*

6. *You are blamed for things you didn't do. But I don't know this for certain.*

7. *You like me a lot.*

Mom is heading out here. I can hear her coming down the back steps although I can't see anything from the window since I'm sitting down. So I close the notebook and pick up *Sounder*, which I've already read.

She opens the door to the shed and comes in.

"I'm on my way to school for tryouts for *The Sound of Music*. Want to come with me?"

Every summer she puts on a musical with the high school students and they practice all summer and then have performances in early August and usually I go to all of them after I get back from camp.

"No, thank you," I say coolly.

She's picking up her little cardboard pots, which have dropped on the floor, lining them up on one of the shelves, pretending to be interested in her pots although I know she's about to say something *important*.

She's facing me now, one foot on a stool, her hands in her jeans pockets, her curly hair frizzy in the dampness. Looking up at her from the floor, she's very tall and skinny and I look more like my father, who's her height, maybe a little shorter.

"It's too bad Tommy Bowers had to go to New York," she says, "out of the blue," as Puss would say.

I draw my knees up under my chin, a sense of relief rushing through me.

"I didn't know he'd gone to New York."

New York. And all the time she knew and maybe even my father knew and no one thought to tell me.

"His grandfather died last Sunday," Mom says. "Clarissa's father."

"So he's gone all week?" I ask.

"Probably until Friday." She shoves the stool against the wall and heads out the door. "No television, El. On your honor."

I don't answer.

I've been "on my honor" since I can remember and always wonder what being on my honor really means. It doesn't mean I won't watch television at all while she's gone. I can't imagine she believes that. It's strange the way parents ask their kids not to do something, all the time knowing that they will. It drives me crazy.

But sitting here in the potting shed, it occurs to me, like a light flash in my brain, that since I *do* watch TV when my parents are gone and they probably know there's no way to stop me if they're not here, I can also *refuse* to go to camp. They can't exactly *make* me.

"Mom," I call as I jump up from the floor and rush to the door. She's halfway across the yard and turns around, her expression sour.

"Impudent" is her word to describe the way I sometimes speak to her. It's been the same since I was little and I've never looked up "impudent" in the dictionary or asked her what she means by it. But I can guess.

She has one hand on the railing of our back porch.

"Why didn't you tell me where Tommy was?"

She shrugs and turns to go up the steps. "Because you didn't ask," she says.

My face goes suddenly hot and I can feel my temper boiling over and I can't help myself.

"Should there be any confusion," I say, using the same words my mother has used with me a million times when she's angry, "I will not be going to Camp Farwell in Wells River, Vermont, this summer at all."

13. Unexpected Trouble

It's nearly three on Friday afternoon when Tommy gets back from New York, a light rain falling, soft summer air blowing across the city. I'm sitting on the front porch writing him the same letter I was writing him a few days ago when a yellow cab pulls up to the curb in front of the Bowerses' house and Tommy hops out first.

I reposition myself on the porch railing so he'll be able to see me if he looks in my direction—balancing with my feet against the railings, pretending to read over the letter I'm writing to him.

"Ellie!" He's shouting now and I look up as if I'm surprised by his sudden reappearance and there he is, already running toward my house waving his arms.

"I couldn't call you," he says, stopping short of falling into my arms, the way it happens in the old-time movies. "I didn't know your telephone number and Clarissa kept crying about her father and so I didn't want to ask her if she knew it." He hops up on the railing across from me.

"I thought you'd disappeared," I say.

"I was sure you'd think that." He takes a green-striped candy stick out of his pocket and hands it to me. "I got it for you at the airport."

"I'm sorry about your grandfather," I say.

"It's okay. It was only the second time I'd seen him." He slips out of his shoes. "I mean I didn't see him, of course, because he'd already been cremated."

"I went to my grandfather's funeral when I was eight and there was only music and praying. I don't remember any speeches."

"I thought it would be creepy but funerals aren't so bad." He takes another candy stick from his pocket and tears off the cellophane. "I would have have liked to see a body since I never have but there was a big party afterward and I had a red wine and met a lot of relatives I didn't know I had."

He checks his watch, jumps off the railing, and hurries down my front steps.

"We've got to hurry," he says. "It's after three and we need to get the lollipops for tomorrow."

The shopping center is on Pageant Street about four blocks from our house. There's a grocery store and a five-and-ten and a hamburger and pasta restaurant and a drugstore and Wake Up Little Suzie and a dress store for large-size women but nothing for normal-size ones. We hurry up the hill.

Tommy's in a cozy mood, walking along beside me so close he keeps bumping into my shoulder.

"So I have an Aunt Eva who's Clarissa's sister and then her husband who's in a wheelchair and they have two children, very stuck-up, especially the girl who's our age. And then there's an uncle who sounds as if he's swallowed a bag of marbles. Yoble, yoble, yoble." He imitates the sound. "And his wife who divorced him but liked my grandfather even though she didn't like his son."

His slips his arm through mine in that funny way grown-ups have of walking along together. I like it, of course, but it feels a little awkward and embarrassing.

"A bunch of my new cousins were interested to meet me since I'm new to the family and adopted and have this reputation for trouble."

I'm thinking it's weird to suddenly, out of nowhere, have this huge family you've never met. Our family is tiny, only me and Milo and three cousins, one of whom I like okay and the other two are creeps.

"So are you listening?"

"I'm listening," I say.

"The boy cousin—his name is Sean—asked me if I'd ever been in a home for juveniles. I suppose he meant criminals."

"Where did he get that idea?"

"Because his parents were probably talking about how Clarissa had adopted a teenage juvenile delinquent." This seems to please him as he saunters along beside me, shaking his head so his floppy hair is out of his eyes. "And maybe she has," he adds.

"My mother heard good things from the kids in the neighborhood about the Lollipop Garden," I say, changing the subject.

"Good," Tommy said. "I expected that."

"Ms. O'Shaunessey was very excited and so was Hannah's mother and someone else who saw my mother at the grocery store."

When the light turns green, Tommy heads across the street taking hold of my hand.

"By tomorrow afternoon, people will be talking about us in every house on Lincoln Road." He jumps and hits a tree branch, grabbing a handful of leaves.

At the corner, we stop at Wake Up Little Suzie and I show Tommy the sparkly necklace which is still in the window.

"The one you got me is more beautiful," I say.

"Because this one is fake." Tommy's nose is pressed against the storefront window.

We head on down the street past the grocery store and the hamburger restaurant and through the glass doors of the five-and-ten.

G.C. Murphy's is my favorite store in the world. It has everything anyone needs and lots of stuff we don't need, too. And it's cheap enough for me to afford to buy things on my five-dollar weekly allowance. There's makeup and clothes and school supplies and candy and junk food and costumes and masks and wigs and shoes and paintings and rugs and towels and books and toys. I could go on and on.

I know we won't go straight for the candy aisle. It's too much fun to wander the aisles back and forth imagining what you'd buy even though you won't.

In the cosmetics department, Tommy checks the powders and blush and nail polish. He picks up a tube of Raspberry lipstick, takes off the top, and winds out the lipstick.

"Do you like this color?" he asks.

"I don't know. I can't tell without trying it."

"Try it," he says.

I laugh. "Then I'll have to buy it."

"Just try it," Tommy says. "You don't have to buy it if you don't like the color."

"I do, Tommy," I say. "If I try it on, I'll get my germs on it and then I have to buy it so no one else will get my germs."

He looks at me with an odd expression.

"Who will know?" he asks.

I consider this question. I've never thought this way before, and although I know it's wrong to use something without buying it, I wonder how a person knows something is wrong if he doesn't know the rules. Or whether someone like Tommy knows what Puss refers to as "the difference between right and wrong."

"I'll know," I say in answer to his question. "I'll know I have germs and have left them on the lipstick and someone will buy it and take it home and put it on with my germs spread all over her lips."

"That's how many germs you've got?" he asks. "Thanks for telling me. I'll be more careful after this."

We go down the costume aisle and Tommy picks up a skeleton mask. He puts on the mask and looks at himself in the mirror, making a strangling gesture with his hands at his neck. I'm trying on a black mask with silver sequins and pressing my face into the skeleton on Tommy's face when a clerk appears out of nowhere and tells us to return the masks and not to try them on unless we plan to buy them.

I quickly take off the mask and put it back in the bin of black-and-sequin masks, but Tommy is in no hurry. While the clerk watches with one hand on her hip, her lips tight, her eyes so narrow they've almost disappeared into her head, Tommy makes a drama of taking off his skeleton mask, reaching behind him, pulling the rubber band, lifting the skeleton face very slowly off his own face, waving it in the air to shake off the germs, putting it back in the bin.

"Don't let me see that again," the clerk says.

"Don't look," Tommy says.

But I'm worried.

"Let's leave and come back through another door," I whisper.

"We have no reason to leave. We did nothing wrong."

I can tell he has a plan as we head to the candy department.

"How much money do you have?" he asks.

"I forgot about money." I reach into the pocket of my shorts and find four quarters, a dime, and a penny, which I hold out in my palm for him to see.

"That's it," I say. "What about you?"

"Nothing," he says, pulling the pockets of his trousers inside out.

"Then we should go back home and get some money," I say, knowing that I've got at least twenty-seven dollars in my top bureau drawer, ready to go into my savings account at the bank.

But Tommy has something else in mind.

We reach the candy aisle, rows and rows of large bags of chocolates and jellybeans and jellies and licorice and nut candy and bars and gummy bears and lollipops. I don't like candy except peanut M&M's. So aisles of candy actually make me feel a little sick and I hang behind Tommy while he walks up and down the aisle, looking around from time to time, picking up a candy bar and looking at the contents, the calories and ingredients, that sort of thing, as if he has an interest in such details.

I'm getting impatient since it's taking so long to look at candy that we won't be able to buy because of our money problem. And I'm worried that at any moment the clerk will see us loitering and take us to the manager, who will call the police, who will come to the five-and-ten and pick us up in the paddy wagon and take us to the police station and call our parents.

All of this is going through my mind when Tommy tells me he's ready to leave.

"Home?"

He nods and leads the way in a kind of hurry out of the store.

"Are we going to get money?" I ask.

He shakes his head.

"The clerk was a creep," he says.

"I know," I say.

We are headed down Lincoln and Tommy's walking so fast that I have to jog to keep up.

"We should check on our club," he says as we reach the Watsons' corner. "I haven't been here all week. Have you?"

"I didn't want to come without you."

We walk up the driveway, looking in the window for the Miss Watsons but no one is visible. Tommy pushes the lattice gate very gently since it's almost off its hinges. He shuts the door behind us, opens the beach chairs, and we sit down.

"What time do you have to be home?"

"Soon," I say. "My parents have been away all day and they'll expect me to go swimming at the neighborhood pool with them and then get pizza."

"Do we have time to plant the lollipops?" he asks, leaning back in his chair, his arm behind his neck.

"Before I have to be home?"

"That's the question," he says.

I'm confused. As far as I know, we don't have any lollipops to plant unless Tommy plans for us to get some money and go back to G.C. Murphy's and it's too late for me to do that.

"I can't be home any later than five."

"Good," he says.

And he reaches into the deep pockets of his trousers and pulls out two bags of lollipops, one from each pocket.

14. Reflection

I've been awake all night. The moon is a circle of light filling my room with a kind of silvery whiteness. I can even see the numbers on my alarm clock. Three in the morning and I'm not even sleepy, so I get up and wander around my bedroom in the white darkness, going finally to the sunporch, where there's a soft breeze. I bring my pillow, drop it onto the cot that faces the Bowerses' house, and lie down.

When Tommy took out the bags of lollipops he had stolen from G.C. Murphy's, I didn't even let him know that I was upset. I acted as if the lollipops had magically materialized in his pockets, like the ones we planted in careful rows for the neighborhood kids to find tomorrow morning.

I don't know what's the matter with me. Certainly I was afraid the clerk at G.C. Murphy's had seen him, seen us leave the store with stolen goods. But I said nothing, as if I approved of what he'd done, as if stealing were the most normal thing in my world.

I helped him plant the lollipops in perfect rows, folded the beach chairs, told him it was time for me to leave, and we left with Tommy talking about our plans for tomorrow morning.

"You're so quiet," Tommy said to me on the walk down the Watsons' driveway and home.

"I guess I am," I said.

But I didn't tell him why and I don't think he worried about my silence or wondered why I was quiet or even if I thought shoplifting was wrong. He needed lollipops and so he took them. Maybe he would have paid for them if we'd had money. Or maybe not.

But I didn't say *anything*, so now I'm so furious at myself for keeping silent, and at Tommy because he might have ruined everything, that I can't sleep.

I don't know what he's thinking. Probably nothing except about tomorrow when the kids arrive under the Watsons' porch, and we turn into magicians.

I got home last night just as my parents were packing up the swimsuits and towels, and we all headed to the swim club and messed around even though it was still raining a light misty rain, and then we went to the pizza parlor for dinner.

We sat at the table and talked about what we'd done all day, and I actually told the truth that I'd gone to the shopping center with Tommy. Just in case the clerk at the five-and-ten had seen him take the lollipops, I wanted to tell the truth that I'd been there, too. I wanted to protect him in spite of what he did and later, sitting with my family at the pizza parlor, I had a sense of doom—a kind of cloud over my head covering the sun so the air around me was cool. And I knew something unpleasant could happen to Tommy and me.

Tommy is sleeping. The lights are off in his room although in another upstairs room they are on and I imagine that Clarissa is still awake. I'm lying on the cot going over and over the day from the moment the taxicab pulled up in front of the Bowerses' house to late afternoon when

Tommy stood up from the beach chair under the Watsons' porch and dumped the lollipops he'd stolen on the ground.

I can't decide whether I'm afraid because what Tommy did was wrong or I'm afraid of being caught and of my parents' disappointment in me, which is worse than anger. I don't remember ever having this jumble of feelings in my brain, as if my skin no longer fits me and I need to squiggle out of it and get a larger size.

Yesterday I was certain of things. I knew what was right to do and what was wrong and never thought about it. Sometimes I did wrong things but I knew they were wrong and that I might be caught and punished. But I made a choice. That's gone now, just dissolved in the air and my brain is in a jumble.

Tonight is not the first time I've thought about right and wrong—really thought about it in a serious way. My father and mother are always arguing about black and white and gray. Mom tends to see the world as good and bad and right and wrong and black and white.

"Things are never black or white, Meg," my father will say. "There're extenuating circumstances or ambiguities or complications. Almost always."

"A person can't live that way," my mother will say.

"Don't be such a teacher!"

And sometimes, my quiet father will slam down the paper or bang the door and leave the room.

I always tend to think like Mom because it's safe to think that way, I guess. Safe and simple. But I'm more interested in what my father has to say.

"Look at the whole picture," he'll say to my mother about such and such a kid at school. "He may have done a bad thing, but it doesn't make him a bad boy. You know that."

And my mother does know that but she's too stubborn to change her mind in front of him.

I don't think Tommy's bad. Not a criminal or a juvenile delinquent or even a bad boy. I know that if I were blamed as an accomplice to his stealing, he would say I hadn't seen him do it, so it wasn't my fault.

My guess is that Tommy's had such an empty life, if he finds something he needs, like lollipops, he takes them.

At least that's what I'm telling myself tonight as I drift off to sleep in the cot on the sunporch with the weight of all this thinking.

Sometime later, still in absolute darkness except for the moon, the light in Tommy's room goes on and that wakes me up. I sit up on the cot and see him across the divide. He's opening the window in his bedroom, leaning out, calling my name.

"Ellie," he calls.

I don't answer.

"Ellie? Can you hear me?"

I lie very still on the cot and hope he can see me in the dark and know that I'm not answering him on purpose.

"I'm so excited, I can't sleep," he says.

And though I want more than anything to run over to the screen on his side of the sunporch, I close my eyes and don't move.

15. Opening Ceremony

Milo is standing beside the cot, fully dressed for the day in his bathing suit and T-shirt, looking down at me and calling my name.

"I'm sleeping," I say. "It's too early to get up."

"It's already six and it's Saturday and it's raining."

I sit up, rubbing my eyes. It's gray and drizzling and warm.

"What about the lollipops? Will they still be growing?"

"They're probably full-grown lollipops by now and the rain won't hurt them. They're under the Watsons' porch."

"I know," Milo says, sitting down on the bed beside me. "How come you slept on the sunporch?"

"I wanted to," I say, stretching, climbing out of bed, checking Tommy's room for the shadow of him getting up but seeing nothing.

"I can hear you talk to Tommy at night," Milo says.

Milo's bedroom is next to mine. He keeps the window open on the side of the house next to the sunporch, so it must be Tommy's side of the conversation that he's heard.

It worries me that Milo is part of the Lollipop Garden. In a funny way, it doesn't bother me to pretend to the neighborhood kids that we can actually grow lollipops. But it does bother me with my very own brother. I suppose it feels like a betrayal because Milo trusts me absolutely. And he should. I'm his sister.

I grab my clothes out of the bottom drawer of my dresser, the same clothes I wore yesterday, including my yellow cargo shorts, and go into the bathroom to change. I can tell Milo is standing on the other side of the door. I can see his feet.

Everything is ready under the Watsons' porch, so Tommy and I have nothing to do. I'm bringing the games, board games that we keep in the television room, and I'm picking up another packet of Mom's new seeds from the potting shed to pass out for next week's lolli-pops. Tommy's making lemonade and I made chocolate chip cookies after we got home last night from the pizza parlor. We're doing a story game that Tommy made up, pretending we're orphans. I've never wanted to be an orphan at all, but Tommy tells me that most ordinary kids do.

"Orphans-on-the-Go." That's Tommy's name for us.

Milo is standing right beside the door to the bathroom when I open it.

"Can I come with you and Tommy to the Lollipop Garden?" he asks.

"We have to go first and get everything ready for camp and then you come at ten with the other kids."

"But I'm your brother." He follows me downstairs.

"It doesn't make any difference, Milo," I say. "You're the camper and I'm the counselor."

He follows me into the kitchen, sitting down at the table, his chin on his fists.

"I don't like that."

"That's the way it is if you want to be part of the Lolli-pop Garden."

He reaches for a chocolate chip cookie.

"No cookies for breakfast," I say, but he eats one anyway and takes another.

I pour cereal for us both, slice two bananas, get the orange juice out of the fridge, and sit down for breakfast.

"I hope my lollipops grew in purple," Milo says. "It's my favorite color."

"I hope so, too," I say. "Do you remember which seeds are yours?"

"Mine are on the bottom of the first row," he says.

"Maybe we should have put a sign with the kids' names next to the seeds," I say. "What do you think?" I ask Milo. "Everyone may not have as good a memory as you do."

"They will remember exactly. They were paying attention," he says, and then his eyes light up. "Do you hear Tommy on the front porch."

"Already? It isn't even seven."

Milo nods.

And he's right.

My mom and dad are up and Milo runs upstairs to talk to them. I call goodbye, tell them I'm headed to camp, and Tommy and I hurry out the back door. We stop at the potting shed where I grab some carrot seeds, and then head out the gate, down the driveway, and up the street to the Watsons'.

It's a spitting rain but constant, with a little wind so the rainwater is blowing into our faces.

"You don't think they'll stay home because of the rain?" Tommy's out of breath from carrying the board games and lemonade and cups and cookies and napkins.

"They'll come," I say. "Milo was ready to come with us, he's so excited."

But I can imagine that in other houses the kids are waking up to this damp, gray day, sliding down the steps in their pajamas, and heading for the television to watch cartoons.

The lights are out upstairs in the Brittle house.

"Do you see the twins?" Tommy asks, stopping to look up.

I don't see anyone moving or any lights.

"It's too early," I say.

"I hope," Tommy replies.

It's a little after ten. The snack is set up on a small table Tommy has brought from his house, blankets are spread on the ground, the beach chairs are open, and he and I are standing at the lattice door waiting.

Behind us, the lollipops are blooming in four perfect lines of cellophane. Outside, the weather has picked up. It's raining in sheets.

We don't speak but I know what Tommy is thinking.

"Do you want me to go to the end of the driveway and check if anyone is coming?" I ask.

"I'll come with you," he says.

And I follow him down the drive, stopping at the top of Lincoln Road where the brick wall runs into the Watsons' drive.

Ahead of us, just about at our house, we see a line of yellow raincoats, eight or ten of them at least, walking up the street single file. Passing my house, they stop, and Milo trots down the front steps in his yellow raincoat joining someone—it must be Sean—and then they head up the street toward us like so many yellow ducklings.

We don't stop to check if Anthony and Alexander are coming down their front steps. We run back up the driveway, ducking under the porch, shaking off the rain since we don't have raincoats.

I look over at Tommy and smile. I can't help myself. He has a smile the size of a giant playground.

16. Almost Famous

It's Sunday morning. The bells of the Methodist church around the corner are ringing, and the bells of the Episcopal church on the main avenue are ringing. Up and down Lincoln Road, families are going to church or Sunday school. Some of the families on our block are walking home past my house after Catholic Mass.

Tommy and I are sitting on my front porch drinking lemonade in wineglasses. Milo is with us. He can't keep his eyes off Tommy. In the pocket of his jeans are the five remaining lollipops for the rest of the week, mostly yellows. He is licking a yellow one now.

"This is the best I've ever had in my life," he tells us earnestly. "I guess that's what happens when you plant your own personal seeds."

"Exactly," Tommy says. "It makes all the difference to have personal seeds."

Milo and I are not at church. There is a family reunion of aunts and uncles at Puss's house, and the terrible cousins, including us, aren't invited. So my parents have allowed us to skip Sunday school.

I haven't said anything to Tommy yet about stealing, but I'm going to speak to him and I know what I'm going to say. Yesterday after the lollipop camp was over, I had to go shopping with my mother and Puss. Last night, I went to the movies with Mom. And now Milo is here, so I can't say anything yet. But I will.

Sean and Cara and Ian O'Shaunessey are walking by our house with their parents, and Milo waves and runs down the steps to greet them, throwing his arm around Sean's neck.

"I'm eating my Sunday lollipop," he says to Sean. "Right, Tommy?"

"Right, Milo," Tommy replies.

"I already ate mine," Sean calls to Tommy and me. "A red one. I had a purple yesterday."

"You kids are amazing," Ms. O'Shaunessey calls to Tommy and me. "Mine love the camp."

"I'm glad they do," Tommy says.

"Cara tells me it's magic."

Tommy gives me a look as if to ask if she actually *knows* about the lollipops.

"Well . . . ," he begins.

"Magic is magic," she calls cheerfully, and turns away, walking up the street with Mr. O'Shaunessey, Ian, and Cara, followed by Milo with Sean. "I'm taking Milo home with us for lunch," she calls back.

So now I'm alone with Tommy. My heart is beating, my mouth is dry, and I'm almost ready to change my mind and say nothing about the shoplifting when he starts the conversation.

"I know you were mad that I took the lollipops," he says.

"I was," I say. "And I was mad at myself, too, because I didn't say anything to you about it and just let it happen as if it were okay with me if you shoplift."

He shrugs.

"I've taken stuff from stores before," he says. "Stuff I need. And I've never been caught."

I don't say anything.

"It isn't hard to do."

"But it's wrong," I say. "It's stealing."

"It doesn't hurt anybody. Things that are wrong hurt people. I don't do those things," Tommy says.

I don't want to say too much. Not so much that Tommy decides to end our friendship.

"It's wrong because you shouldn't get something for nothing," he says.

"I guess that's it," I say.

"I'm sorry," he says. "I'm really sorry."

"Me too. I should have told you right away."

The Blocks are on a family bike ride, cycling past our house, and Sarah waves.

"That's Ellie and Tommy," she calls to her mother, who puts on the brakes and slows down and waves to us.

"Great experiment, you guys," she calls.

"Thanks," we say in unison, although I don't exactly know what experiment we're doing. The Lollipop Garden isn't exactly a science class.

Tommy gives me a little jab in the arm.

"Experiment!"

In the distance, I see one of the Brittle twins run down his front steps and head for my house.

"Which one is that?" Tommy asks.

"Alexander," I say.

His face is bright red and bubbly as he runs up our front steps and stops dead in front of us.

"What's up?" Tommy asks.

"Anthony says you can't grow cellophane and sticks and I say he's wrong about that."

"Does he think you can grow candy?" I ask.

"I guess he does," Alexander says.

"I can't explain the details," Tommy says casually. "I know you put the seeds in the ground and the lollipops grow, and when they come out of the dirt, there's cellophane around the candy and sticks. I don't know how that happens but it does."

"So it's just by magic and that's that, right?"

"Right."

"And if Anthony doesn't believe in it, then he can't come any longer to the Lollipop Garden."

"Well . . . ," Tommy begins.

"I want you to call my parents and tell them Anthony can't come because he's ruining things."

"Maybe he'll change his mind."

"I don't think so," Alexander says sadly. "He's too mean."

"Give him a chance," I say. "In the beginning, I didn't believe lollipops could grow from seeds."

Alexander takes a yellow lollipop out of his pocket.

"This is my Sunday one," he says. "I hid Anthony's in the guinea pig cage."

"That's not such a great idea. Something could happen in the guinea pig cage," Tommy says.

"To the lollipop?"

"Who knows? The guinea pig could eat the lollipop and then what?" Tommy says. "And you better go home now before your parents get worried."

My parents pull into the driveway and get out of the car just as Milo comes home from Sean's house. They come around the house and up the steps to the front porch. My heart is beating in my mouth for fear they'll object to Tommy's being here.

"How was dinner?" I ask.

"Fascinating," my father says. He always refers to dinner at Puss's house as fascinating, which even I know he doesn't mean. "Puss wanted to catch the aunts and uncles up on her intestinal problems and her arthritis and the woman she knows, Mrs. Peacock, who dropped dead in church last Sunday during the offertory hymn."

My mother giggles.

"Well, I'm sorry we missed it," I say.

"We weren't invited," Milo says, squiggling into the Adirondack chair with my father. "That's how come we got to miss Sunday school."

"So what are you guys up to?" my father asks.

"Just stuff," I say, glancing at Tommy, hoping he'll jump in with a plan.

"I was hoping that Ellie and I could go to the movies," Tommy says.

He's leaning against the porch railing and seems for all the world to be as comfortable with us as if we were his family. I give him a quizzical look. I think he knows how my parents feel about him.

"A new family comedy called *Oatmeal* is playing at the mall," he says. "And I thought we could go to the five o'clock show."

My father looks at my mother. "Meg?"

"I don't see any reason why not," she says. "If you change out of those appalling shorts, El."

"How come?" I ask. I'm wearing my yellow cargo shorts.

"They're dirty, for one."

"I like those navy blue pants you had on last Sunday, the ones with buttons down both sides," my father says.

"Those are a good choice," my mother says.

I hate the navy pants. They make me look like pudding, but I put them on anyway with a white T-shirt with "hell-o!" written in red script on the front. I grab a sweater and run down the steps. Milo is waiting at the bottom.

"Have fun, guys," Milo says, waving sadly. "I haven't gotten to see *Oatmeal* yet."

"Yes you have, Milo," I say. "At least twice."

"But I forget it already."

I'm not about to take Milo with us, so I wave goodbye and hop down the front steps, and off I go with Tommy Bowers, walking down the street side by side. I can hardly believe my good luck.

"I'm glad you told me the truth," I say when we're beyond my parents' hearing.

"About what?"

"Shoplifting."

"I won't do it again," he says.

"How can you be sure?" I ask.

"I don't need to do it anymore," he says.

And I believe him.

17. Kiss Me on Second Avenue

We turn right at the bottom of our steps and head down the hill toward Vanderbilt Avenue, where the mall is located. I've never walked to the mall but I've been here a million times to the movie theater, which has four screens showing on the weekend. One screen shows a children's movie, one shows foreign films with English subtitles, and the other two are just regular films. We go as a family most Sunday evenings and sometimes have popcorn instead of dinner, and then if it isn't too late, we stop for ice cream sundaes with whipped cream afterward. Usually the O'Shaunesseys are there when we are and we sit with them. I'm hoping the O'Shaunesseys have plans to stay at home tonight, but as we cross the avenue I see their van pull into the parking lot at the mall. You can't miss their van, which is bright red with "O'SHAUNESSEY" in black letters written on the back as if they think of themselves as a rock band.

"They're probably seeing *Oatmeal*, too," I say.

"That's okay," Tommy says. "We don't need to talk to the O'Shaunesseys because we're not seeing *Oatmeal*."

I catch my breath. I should have known that we weren't going to see a children's movie. It's just like Tommy to say one thing and plan to do another.

"I've already seen *Oatmeal*," he says.

"Me too," I say. "Once with Milo and once with my mom and once with P.J. for her birthday."

"We're going to see *Kiss Me on Second Avenue*."

"Good," I say, and though I've never heard of this movie, I can tell from its name that it's rated R or PG-13 and I'm probably too young to get a ticket. I can't tell if I'm about to be sick or if I'm so excited my stomach has turned suddenly into a dance club.

"Don't worry. I've done this a lot," Tommy says.

"R-rated movies?"

"Many times. By myself. It's a piece of cake."

I follow him into a yogurt shop and order a vanilla cone with chocolate jimmies to share.

"And you're not worried about buying a ticket and lying about your age?" I ask, holding up the cone so he can have a lick.

"What can happen?"

"Trouble."

Tommy shakes his head. "I buy the ticket. If they ask me how old I am, I say, *'Old? Seexteen zees month. Identifica-tion? I don't know theees word "identification," ' I say." He runs his fingers through his long hair. "And then the guy selling the tickets shakes his head and says, 'Forget it, man,' and in I go."

It's not that my parents are strict about movies. I've been to plenty of R movies with them and they don't worry that my mind will be warped or my little heart destroyed. What I'm worried about now as we walk into the Loew's Toledo and head over to the popcorn and the ticket booth is the O'Shaunesseys. I'm sure they're here with all their kids and probably the cousins since the cousins usually come to the movies, and I'm sure they're planning to see *Oatmeal*. If Ms. O'Shaunessey happens to see me walk into *Kiss Me on Second Avenue*, she'll call Mom. That's the kind of mother she is. She believes it's her duty to let every parent and teacher know exactly what other children, not her own, are doing wrong. All in a very upbeat voice, with a big smile and a clap on the back. But, as my father says, she's a little too interested in a ticket to heaven for his taste.

The poster for *Kiss Me on Second Avenue* says R and not for a moment am I going to be able to pass for seventeen even in my navy trousers and white T-shirt.

"We can't do this," I say. "I thought it was PG-13."

Tommy smiles with this patient expression as if it takes all of the energy he has to spend an afternoon with me.

"Don't worry. Just stand beside me and you'll see what's up."

I do stand beside him but I'm too worried to talk, all the while looking around for one of the O'Shaunesseys or even my parents. It would be just like my mom to say to my dad, "Let's just go to the movies and meet up with Ellie." And my dad would say sure. He seldom argues.

When it's our turn, Tommy asks for two tickets to *Oatmeal*.

"*Oatmeal?*" I ask as we leave the line and head for the popcorn.

Tommy raises his eyebrows, rolls his eyes.

"Just watch," he says. "Don't say anything. Do what I do."

We get popcorn and ginger ale in cups large enough to sleep in. We go over to the poster for *Kiss Me on Second Avenue* and read the reviews. The review I read, a long one with four stars, says the story is a love affair, heartbreaking and sweet, that takes place in the midst of gang violence, sex scenes, and frontal nudity.

My breath is suddenly thin, my mouth is dry, and I'm wondering what Tommy has in mind. I know *Oatmeal* is not what he's planning to see, but I can't imagine how we're going to see this heartbreaking love affair with sex scenes and nudity without getting caught.

Out of the corner of my eye, I see the O'Shaunesseys. They're in front of us, now giving their tickets to the person at the entrance, now walking down the corridor. We follow, several people behind. I see Cara and Ian and Sean slip into theater three, where *Oatmeal* is playing. I grab Tommy by the elbow and whisper to him to wait, and we lean flat against the wall letting the crowds stream by us.

Then we hurry down the corridor past the foreign film at theater one, past the feature film called *SpaceWalk*, past *Oatmeal* in theater three, and past Ms. O'Shaunessey standing outside the theater talking to a tall, skinny woman older than Puss.

"Where're we going?" I whisper.

"Just follow. Look like it's perfectly normal."

No one is at the door to theater four with *Kiss Me on Second Avenue*. Tommy walks in, takes a seat halfway down and on the aisle, and I follow, climbing over his legs, slipping down in my seat so just the top of my head shows above it.

I look over at Tommy and he's smiling as the previews begin and the lights dim, smiling so the dimples in his cheek are little craters next to his lips.

He turns and looks at me.

"I'm very honored you are here with me, Eleanor Tremont," he says, and I smile, too, a giggle slipping up from someplace in my chest. I put my feet on the seat, press my face into my knees, and bury the laughter in my arms.

"Honored to be with you, too," I say.

18. Discovered

My mother is sitting on my bed when I run up the steps after the movie and burst into my bedroom.

"Hi," I say. "What's up?"

That's what my father says when he comes home or calls on the phone, and I say it now because I *know* something is up. My mother is not in good humor and I don't *want* to know what it's about.

"I had a great time," I say, hoping to deflect her question, certain that she's waiting to talk to me because she's discovered some trouble. So, I decide to do the talking.

Yakkity yak, blah, blah, blah, this and that. My mom just sits there looking at me.

I step out of my trousers and hang them up, which I wouldn't do under normal circumstances, circumstances in which my mother is not sitting on my bed waiting to ask me a question I don't want to hear. It's only eight o'clock but I'm thinking it might be a good idea to seem *very* tired, to put on my pajamas and hurry downstairs for Sunday night TV, which we sometimes watch together.

I catch a glimpse of my mother out of the corner of my eye. She's wearing shorts and an oversized T-shirt, probably gym clothes, which means she's just gotten back from working out. Her bare feet are crossed at the ankles and she has something or seems to have something in her hand.

"So we went first to the yogurt place and I had vanilla with jimmies and then to the movie place and got popcorn and watched the film and walked home and met up with P.J.'s parents on the way. They say P.J. *hates* camp." I decide that the constant talking is working. This way, Mom doesn't have a chance to say very much herself.

And she doesn't. I'm on the floor checking a mosquito bite on my ankle that I got on the walk home, which I scratched and now it's bleeding.

I look over at my mother, who's sitting very still, watching me.

"I'm going to watch TV with Milo," I say, and turn to leave.

"Just a moment, Ellie. I need to ask you something first."

The light is on beside my bed, a ballerina lamp although I never was a ballerina nor ever wished to be one. It's gotten dark out, not black but dusk, and there're shadows across the floor of my bedroom. My mother has changed positions. Her arm is lifted, her palm up in a gesture of offering, and on her palm is something familiar.

"Do you know where this came from?" she asks.

She's holding the teardrop-diamond necklace Tommy gave me for my birthday. I lean against the wall, suddenly weak.

I can't remember where I must have left it. The other day when Milo climbed in bed with me, I slipped it under the sheets. But today I think I left it in my underwear drawer, under the clothes, so she must have gone looking for it. I have to be calm since I don't know whether I'm going to tell her the truth and am trying to take deep breaths while I make a decision.

"I was putting away your laundry, straightening up your underwear drawer, and I found this under your new camp panties."

I'm sensible enough to know that I can't lie about it now. The necklace certainly couldn't have gotten in my underwear drawer by magic, so I wait for the next question.

"What are you going to tell me?" she asks quietly.

I take a breath and hope there are words waiting when I start to speak.

"Tommy gave it to me for my birthday," I say.

"He did." It's a statement, so she must know already that he gave it to me.

I nod.

"This is the present you meant when you told me that P.J. had left a present on the front porch for your birthday."

"Yes." I slip down to the floor. "I didn't tell you because you didn't want to know."

"I understand why you would have thought that," she says.

"You never liked Tommy Bowers," I say.

"Did he tell you that he took this necklace from his mother's jewelry box?"

I take a deep breath and let my eyelids collapse over my burning eyes so I don't have to see her.

"Do you remember the police at the Bowerses' house the other day?"

"Yes."

"They were there because someone had stolen Clarissa's necklace from her jewelry box." She hesitates for a moment and then gets up from the bed, walks over to where I'm sitting, and drops the necklace in my lap.

"They're real diamonds, you know," she says.

"That's why he wanted me to have it," I say. "Because they're real."

She's standing now, leaning against the closet door, her arms folded across her chest.

"What's going to happen?" I ask, already thinking of what I'll need to take with me when I run away from home.

"Now you're going to call Tommy and tell him what has happened and explain that you have to tell Clarissa and want to tell her with him, and then I'll come with you to the Bowerses so you can return the necklace."

"I don't want you to come with me," I say.

"That's fine," she says. "But you have to talk to Tommy now and go over right away."

I put the necklace around my neck, fasten the clasp, and look at myself in the mirror.

"I don't know why you never liked Tommy," I say.

She hesitates, answering carefully.

"It's true I worried about Tommy but I was also beginning to like him."

"You should trust me," I say to her. "I'm your daughter."

She doesn't reply to this but I can tell just by the expression on her face that she is thinking about what I said.

"Eleanor?" She stops to open the bedroom door. "Did Tommy tell you where he got the necklace?"

I'm not sure what to say. I'm not going to tell her that he *told* me he bought it at a jewelry store. And I won't say I don't know where he got it, either.

It's better for me to say nothing than to betray Tommy.

"Perhaps you ought to take the necklace off," my mother says.

I turn away, heading for the sunporch.

"Not yet," I reply.

19. The Sunporch

I'm sitting on one of the cots on the sunporch and Milo is sleeping in the cot next to me, the covers over his head so my flashlight doesn't keep him awake. I'm writing a letter to Tommy, who I can see through the window straight across from me. He's been sent to his room, probably for the rest of his life.

Tommy and I have plans to run away tomorrow morning as soon as his parents leave the house. But sitting here next to Milo, I know that I can't leave him alone in the house without me. So I'm trying to figure a way we can keep the Lollipop Garden without running away from home.

*   *   *

Things didn't go well at the Bowerses' house tonight. I went over by myself, carrying the diamond necklace in a plastic baggie and Tommy met me on the front porch.

"Are you mad at me?" he asked first off.

"I'm not at all mad," I said, which was true. "I liked that you wanted me to have a beautiful necklace."

He opened the screen door and I followed him into the living room, where Clarissa was sitting on a small pink flowered chair with her legs crossed and Mr. Bowers was reading the Sunday paper in a large chair with a footrest. Clarissa watched us cross the room but Mr. Bowers seemed to be more interested in the sports section than in our criminal activity and didn't look up until I handed the necklace to Clarissa and sat down next to Tommy.

"Pretty swell jewelry for a— What is it you are, thirteen years old?"

Tommy gave me a funny look. "Twelve," I said.

"I've already spoken with Tommy," Clarissa began, and for some reason, I couldn't take my eyes off her very sharp, narrow nose, which seemed to be growing as I watched. "And I believe you are really free of involvement in this necklace ordeal, isn't that right?"

"I don't know what you mean," I said, watching the way

her nostrils flared when she spoke as if they were made of such thin material that the slightest movement of air made them billow.

"Tommy gave you a present and told you he'd purchased it at a jewelry store, isn't that correct?"

I don't think I like Clarissa. Other people like her and my mother thinks she's fair and kind, but she seems prissy to me.

"So, thank you for bringing back the necklace and there's no need for you to linger. The necklace is my problem with Tommy."

"Except," I said, "I knew from the start that he'd borrowed the necklace from your jewelry box."

Looking over at Tommy with his chin out and his head high, so young and proud and strong, I wanted to be in trouble with him.

"Ahhhhh," Clarissa said, drawing hard on the *h*. "That puts another light on things."

Soon my parents were in the Bowerses' living room and Mr. Bowers had put away the sports page and Tommy's punishment of solitary confinement had been levied and the Lollipop Garden had been closed down by proclamation of the Bowers family.

"Somehow, El," my mother said as we walked across the

driveway that separates our house from the Bowerses', "I don't believe you did know about the necklace."

I didn't reply.

"I think you were protecting Tommy," she said.

"I love Tommy Bowers," Milo said. He was waiting for us in the driveway.

I was glad of this. Milo was an outside observer, as my father would say, an innocent bystander. He had nothing to gain by coming to Tommy's defense, so maybe my mother would listen to him.

"I don't want to close the Lollipop Garden," I said. "I don't understand why Clarissa can make us do that."

"She's trying to find a punishment for Tommy equal to the harm she feels he's caused," my mother said, and by the way she spoke I could tell she didn't agree.

"Maybe you should tell her to be nice to him, extra nice," I said. "He's not had very good luck with mothers."

"That's true."

We sat in the kitchen while Mom made lemonade from scratch. "But he does have a habit of getting into trouble like this. Like stealing."

"I don't think of what he did as stealing," I said.

"He took something that didn't belong to him," she replied. "That's stealing."

"He's never had things and never had money, so he's had to learn how he can have things that he wants to have."

"But it's wrong."

I fold my arms across my chest, unwilling to argue.

"Have you ever seen him steal anything else?" my mother asked.

"Never," I replied.

"Ellie?"

I finished my lemonade and went upstairs to bed.

Which is where I am now sitting, on a cot on the sunporch with a sleeping Milo, writing a letter to Tommy.

Dear Tommy,

We will figure out a way so we don't have to close down the Lollipop Garden. We have to keep it for the sake of the kids. They need us. And I'm not at all mad about the diamond necklace and how it got to be mine and then had to go back to Clarissa's jewelry box even though I know she never wears it.

Just to let you know, I've saved fifteen dollars of my allowance to buy lollipops to plant for next Saturday and that's enough candy to last us until the end of July, so you don't have to worry anymore about having enough because I do and will give it to you and that's that.

I've got a lot of things I've been thinking about but I'll wait till next time we see each other tomorrow or run away to wherever, maybe New York because Alaska is so far. And cold. Please call me pronto.

Love, Eleanor Russell Tremont

Tommy must have noticed the flashlight moving around on the sunporch because he's standing by the window. The window is closed and he's making no effort to open it, just standing there looking in my direction but not at me although I've turned the light of the flashlight toward my face so he can see that it's me.

I wave and call his name but softly. I certainly don't want my parents to wake up. Or, especially, the Bowerses.

But Tommy just stands there for a while, a shadow, an outline of a boy, and then he turns and climbs back into bed, shutting off the light.

20. Under the Watsons' Porch

It's Saturday, the last Saturday in June, the second week in which lollipops have grown in the garden and there're eighty-four of them glittering in the sunlight streaming through the lattice under the Watsons' porch.

Tommy and I are stretched out on the beach chairs and he has an unlit pipe between his lips. We haven't been talking since we got here, which was early morning, but we were later than we'd planned and had to plant the lollipops. Besides, we talked all week, every day, sitting in the potting shed or at the counter of M&J

Root Beer on Vanderbilt Avenue or on my front porch or on Tommy's. Clarissa put out some porch furniture for us and made cookies and limeade and said she wanted us to make ourselves comfortable.

Perhaps he was beginning to like her better than he had.

"Clarissa is a good woman, Ellie," Mom said to me the night after the crime discovery. "She's trying to be a good mother but she's inexperienced. We have to give her a chance."

"Not my problem," I said. "She's not my mother."

"Well, why don't you help Tommy out with her. He needs to understand that Clarissa is trying."

We were sitting in my bedroom. Mom was on the floor in a yoga position with her legs wrapped around each other, her arms in the air, and her face pointing in the direction of the sun, but that didn't seem to ruin her concentration on our conversation.

"I thought I wasn't supposed to be a friend of Tommy's any longer," I said. "I thought you and Dad decided he was too much trouble."

Mom unwound her legs, rested her arms, and turning to face me, she shook her head. "We've changed our minds," she said, stretching her arms above her head.

"We listened to other people and that was wrong, especially for a couple of teachers who ought to know better that a kid isn't necessarily what you hear about him from other people."

I couldn't believe my ears.

"Tommy's won us over with his good heart," she said.

I didn't argue. Parents are strange people, hardly like regular humans sometimes, and I'm not going to even try to figure them out.

"Does this mean we can keep the Lollipop Garden?"

She looked at me, a sweet, devilish expression on her face, like a girl's.

"You don't need to ask my permission to keep the Lollipop Garden, El," she said. "You're going to keep the Lollipop Garden anyway whatever we say."

"I bought the lollipops in case you were wondering," Tommy says. "I got them yesterday at the five-and-ten, three bags for six dollars, and that saleslady was there and recognized me and asked me to avoid loitering."

I start to say "good boy" like Mom says to Milo but changed my mind.

"I also got you this." He reaches into his shorts pocket

and takes out a small box and hands it to me. "I got it yesterday at Wake Up Little Suzie with my own money."

I know what it is without opening the box, but I take the lid off slowly, making a ceremony of it. My bare arms are shivery and so is the inside of my stomach, a flush of red burning my cheeks like blush.

To Eleanor Russell Tremont from her best friend, Tommy.

The sparkly necklace I had wanted for my birthday is sitting on a mound of yellow tissue paper.

"It's beautiful," I say. "It's the most beautiful necklace I've ever seen."

"And this time," Tommy says, smiling at me, "it's real."

We are beginning to hear the kids in the neighborhood, shouting and laughing and talking as they come up the hill to the Watsons' house. Tommy checks the lollipops, straightening a few that are bending toward the ground, and we stand in the doorway, our shoulders touching, looking down the driveway. There they come, tumbling toward us full of excitement, our little charges, our monkeys, our team.

"Everything worked out, didn't it?" Tommy says, catching my hand in his.

"Perfectly. And I don't even have to go to Camp Farwell tomorrow," I say, looking over at Tommy's face, which is dappled by the light coming through the slats under the Watsons' porch. "I never would have dreamed this garden by myself."

Susan Shreve is the author of several highly acclaimed novels for adults, young adults, and children, including four books about the Bates family: *The Flunking of Joshua T. Bates*, *Joshua T. Bates Takes Charge*, *Joshua T. Bates in Trouble Again*, and *Goodbye, Amanda the Good*, which *Publishers Weekly* described in a starred review as "perceptive and sympathetic. . . . Readers will recognize their problems on every page." Her last novel for Knopf was *Trout and Me*.

Susan Shreve lives in Washington, D.C.